TRACKS

CHANNA WICKREMESEKERA

Fiction

The Bogans
Asylum
In the Same Boat
Distant Warriors
Walls

History

Tough Apprenticeship: Sri Lankan Military against the Tamil Militants 1979 – 1987.

The Tamil Separatist War

Kandy at War: Indigenous Military Resistance to European Expansion in Sri Lanka 1594 - 1818

The Best Black Troops in the World: British Perceptions and the Making of the Sepoy 1746 - 1805.

TRACKS

TRACKS

CHANNA WICKREMESEKERA

Second edition.

Tracks by Channa Wickremesekera

Tracks is a work of fiction

Typeset by Jesse Gordon

Cover designed by Vernon Tissera

ISBN 978-0-646-95800-2

For Disara

Acknowledgements

My thanks go to Don Phillips and Graham Duff for reading the manuscript and commenting on it, Jesse Gordon for his excellent typesetting and designing skills, and Vernon Tissera for his cover design.

PROLOGUE

"Robbie!"

I turned around, startled. It's been nearly six months since I heard that name. And this was the last place I had ever expected to hear it, here on the lawns of the university, surrounded by other young people, laughing, studying, and chatting in the sun. And certainly not after last summer's events. But still, the name was enough to turn my head.

I froze when I saw him, the Robbie in question. Tall, wiry and as blond as they come. And from behind, he looked exactly like him, my Robbie. The same height, the same build, and the same blond hair dancing as he spoke to the girl who had just called out to him.

I stared at him. Can this be true? Was something wonderfully strange and unnatural going on here? Can it really be him? Robbie? My Robbie? Here? At Uni?

Then the boy turned around, and I saw that the face was different. Instead of the full red lips there were two thin strips thatched by a mousy moustache. And no sad baby blue eyes.

No it was not my Robbie. It could never have been.

ONE

"Let's get in," Robbie said, getting up abruptly.

The train came out of the tunnel, lights like big yellow saucers, growing and glowing, wheels screeching as they grated to a halt. We all got up after Robbie, and started walking towards the edge of the platform, waiting for the train to stop and the doors to open.

We have been on the platform since almost six, sitting there, doing nothing as usual. The five of us, four boys and a girl. All teenagers and except me, all mongrels. Robbie, half Scottish, half Aussie, Mark, half Italian, half Aussie, Marty, Half Aussie, half Islander and Sarah a mix of something that has left her dark blond, green eyed and completely batty. Then of course there is me. One hundred percent Sri Lankan, second generation. Not that any of this really mattered to us. We were teenagers.

Trains had come and gone, and dusk had thickened to night. Robbie had not shown the slightest interest in getting on a train. He just sat on the bench, under the light, smoking cigarette after cigarette, staring blankly at the tracks. We sat with him, silent, almost still, as if waiting for him to say something.

Now suddenly a train comes along and Robbie decides he wants to get in.

And when Robbie says we gotta do something, we gotta do it. Always.

Inside the train it's all quiet. Trains are pretty quiet at night on this line during the weekends. Just the odd passenger or two in a carriage, people who obviously had nothing better to do on a Saturday night than nodding off in a train. Strangely, they made the train seem quieter and perhaps even more deserted than it would have appeared if there was nobody on it.

Then, of course, there are teenagers like us. Bored, broke and today in particular, sad.

We were sad because Robbie was sad. He usually is when he comes with a bruised face, a black eye, sometimes a cut lip, gifts from Gary his old man whose idea of stress relief was to smack his boy around. And it was no easy task smacking Robbie around, I tell you. He was not muscly, yes, but tall, wiry and very strong. I have seen him punch guys with chests like blocks of wood and arms like tree trunks and those guys never get a chance to land a punch of their own. But none of them were as big or as mean as Gary I reckon. He was huge, was Gary. And nasty. I have seen him only once but I swear I don't wanna see him again. He must have been at least 6'5" and meaty. You know how kids call big guys tanks? Well, Gary was not just a tank, he was a fucking tanker. And he almost never laughed, I am told. I remember once asking Robbie if Gary ever laughed. Only when I cry, he said.

And today too Robbie had been crying. We could see that. He had been crying before he came to the station, where we usually hung out. His eyes were red and cheeks moist, and the shadow of a nasty bruise smudging that handsome face. And we knew immediately what had happened. You get used to these things. Especially when they happen so frequently.

The train was almost totally deserted. We walked from carriage to carriage. Well, actually Robbie walked and we followed him. But there was hardly anyone. Just a few people here and there, almost everybody half asleep. Robbie just kept walking and the more we walked the more I could sense the rage building in him. We have seen it all too often, usually at times like this. Sadness and defeat turning into anger. It's scary when it happens. And that night too I was scared.

Then it happened. In one of the carriages, I think the last one in the train, there was only one passenger. A man, alone, sitting next to the aisle, facing us but almost asleep. I am not big on recognising ethnic people but this dude looked like an Arab. Fair and dark at the same time. Bushy beard. He probably expected a nice quiet journey back to wherever the hell he was going, and a good kebab with his family. Then maybe a long hot night with his wife.

But then he saw Robbie and Robbie saw him.

Robbie was walking past him, probably to get to the door to get out at the next station when his foot kicked the man in the shins, accidentally I am sure. But it must have hurt like hell and the man cried out in pain and said something to Robbie. Probably something like mind where you are going but because of his accent we couldn't make out anything but an angry voice. But that was all that Robbie needed. He turned around and bashed him.

I wanted to cry out to Robbie not to do it, but then I guess I was too stunned to do anything. It has happened before, a few times, you know he is gonna hurt somebody and you wanna cry out but you can't. And that night it happened again, right before our eyes. By the time I had opened my mouth, Robbie was on to him, punching and kicking.

When Robbie's in this mood it's the scariest fucking thing in the world, I tell you. He goes spastic. Truly spastic. He is kicking and punching yelling shit that doesn't even make sense. And there is no defense. You don't know where his knuckles are gonna land; where the sneakers are gonna connect. You just have to roll in to a ball and hope it will pass. It's a pity he can't do it to Gary. That would have saved Robbie and a lot of other people from bruises and pain. But I guess Gary is too fucking strong for that kinda shit. This is why against Gary Robbie probably rolled into a ball.

The Arab dude also did the same. At first he did not know what was going on. Robbie's fist smacked into his face from nowhere and his head hit against the seat, bouncing like one of those little punching bags on a stand. Then came another punch followed by kicks. He must have received about a dozen punches and kicks before he decided to do the ball thing. But by then his face was so bloody that Robbie's knuckles looked like they were bleeding.

What could we do? All we could do was to try and hold Robbie back, but it's not as easy as saying it. He may not be as strong as Gary but he is still very strong and it took me, Marty and Mark a full minute before we could hold his arms. But even then the legs went kicking at the balled-up Arab on the floor. And Sarah as usual was screaming: "Stop you fucking idiot! Stop! Are you fucking crazy? Stop!!!" That's Sarah for you. Robbie goes spastic, she follows. Nice couple.

And then, we saw her. It was Robbie who saw her first, standing there behind the seat, too terrified to scream. A little Arab girl, no older than six, maybe seven but little, scared shitless, tears streaming down her cheeks, little hands shaking, staring straight at us, too scared to scream or run. Robbie was the first to see her because he stopped. He just stopped in the middle of a kick, frozen, like some weird statue, staring at the girl.

I looked at Robbie and back at the girl. She was still crying, shaking, looking at Robbie and her father on the floor, the balled-up Arab, sobbing like a kid, his face bloody, hands folded over his face.

No one said anything. For how long I don't know. Then, the train came to a halt, somewhere at some dark station and Robbie turned and walked to the door, as abruptly as he had entered the carriage.

We followed. No one looked back at the girl. I guess no one could anymore.

Outside the platform Robbie lit another cigarette, probably his tenth since he met us that evening. I could see his hands, bloody and bruised, shake as they held the lighter to the cigarette, one hand cupping around it to keep the wind away. He drew some smoke and blew it out. He was breathing hard, chest heaving under the windcheater. Next to him Sarah stood, as hysterical as ever.

"How the fuck am I to know there was a girl!" Robbie said, to no one in particular, his voice shaking.

It was Sarah who answered. "You fucking freak!" She screamed at him. "Dumb fucking freak! You nearly killed him! What the fuck were you thinking?"

She was still spastic. Robbie had calmed down in comparison to her. He was still nervous but not nearly as ballistic as he was on the train. But Sarah was nowhere near settling down.

And she was asking a stupid question. Robbie had done it so many times, frequently in her presence. And now she talks as if she was surprised!

Robbie said nothing. Any other time he would have yelled back at her. But not tonight. Not now. He seemed tired, suddenly. All of us were. It had been one fucking hectic night.

"Where the fuck was she all the time? Under the seat?" Mark

asked. He was looking at me, as if scared to speak to Robbie. I just shrugged my shoulders. How the fuck do I know. All I saw was Robbie working over the Arab and then all of a sudden he is frozen shitless, and there, behind the seat, a little girl, crying. Under the seat or inside the seat, fucked if I knew.

"Fucked if I know," I said, simply.

Sarah was still carrying on. "I don't know what is wrong with you. Every fucking week some fucking issue. Can't you think of anything other than bashing people?"

Still Robbie did not answer. Not even a shut the fuck up or I'll bash you too as he would have normally said. Not that he ever bashed her, but it usually shut her up. It was almost as if she needed to be told to shut the fuck up. Loudly and firmly.

But not tonight. Robbie just stood there smoking his fag, staring at the railway track. His hands still shook. Not as much as before but they still shook.

Now we were all silent. Almost still. Sarah too was still now. It was like some fucking funeral or something.

Suddenly there was a loud toot. The train to the city was approaching the opposite platform. Robbie looked at his watch.

"Shit! Almost nine!" He said. "Let's go!" He turned and held out his hand to Sarah. She took it and they both turned around and jumped on the rail track. The train was taking the bend now and we could see its lights hitting the fence to our left. Robbie and Sarah scrambled on to the platform opposite. I swear I could hear Sarah giggling as she slipped and Robbie pulled her up. She loved that kinda shit.

"Cathcya tomorrow," Robbie yelled from the other side. "Sure!" I cried.

The train came to a halt. Another almost empty train. We could now see them inside the carriage. They sat near the window and Sarah was waving at us, blowing us kisses. Robbie too had started smiling again. Only just though.

"They're fucking crazy," Mark said, waving back. "One day they're gonna kill themselves, crossing the tracks like that."

The train started again and was soon gone in the dark. Robbie will get off at the same station Sarah got off at and after saying goodbye to her, will catch the train in the opposite direction to return home. And in the evening we will all meet again. Same time, same platform.

We turned and started walking back. It was ten past nine now. It had been a long night. We were all dead tired even though we had done nothing more than sitting around in silence and holding Robbie in the train.

Outside the station we caught a cab. We all lived close to each other and there was enough change between us to split the short cab ride home. We could have taken a train but no one was in the mood for another train ride. Besides my parents would begin to worry if I am not home in another ten minutes. Dad had called my mobile earlier to say they were going out for something and they'll leave my dinner in the fridge. Still it would be a bad show not to be there when they returned.

We got into the cab and told the driver Mark's address. The man smiled and nodded. He was young; Indian, maybe Sri Lankan. It's hard to tell races in the dark.

"Big night out?" He was trying to make conversation. Or just trying to be sarcastic. But none of us was in the mood for any of that.

"Just shut the fuck up and drive!" Marty ordered.

The rest of the trip was made in silence.

Two

It was late when I woke up the following morning, like 10.30 or something. But it's Sunday. We all get up late on Sunday, except sometimes Dad if he has to finish some work at the garage.

My dad is a mechanic. A bloody good one too, I have heard many people say. He came to Australia from Sri Lanka in the late eighties, to raise a family away from trouble, he says. He had worked in some car joint in Sri Lanka where he was known as a good mechanic. Well, that's what he says and I have no reason to doubt that. People wait for days to get him to work on their cars. They don't trust anybody else. Besides, my dad never lies.

The house we live in was built by him. Well, actually, he bought what was here before and had it renovated. In his own words he found a hovel and made it into a palace. Maybe not exactly a palace, but if you had been here you will know why he calls it so. It's freaking huge. Thick walls, massive rooms. Five of them. All for three people. We were expecting more like you when we built the additional rooms, Dad says sometimes when he wants to tease me. But after seeing you we decided we have had enough. Then he chuckles. He is kinda weird sometimes. He laughs at his own jokes.

Coming back to the house, if you can understand why Dad calls our home a palace if you see it, you will realise straightaway why he is proud of building it if you know what the old house looked like. Dad has kept photos of it taken the day they moved in. Man, I wouldn't call it a hovel. That's way too respectable. Fucking pigsty it was, I tell you. Carpets ripped, paint peeling off walls, holes in the ceiling, the works! Some rooms didn't even have doors, Dad says. But they still moved in because it was cheap and Dad knew he could renovate it. He did some of the renovations himself. Versatile dude, is my dad.

Dad's workshop is just down the road from where we live, in a strip of other workshops and small businesses. It's this big-ass garage with enough room to park four or five vehicles and often, Dad has that many inside and a few outside too. Sometimes Mum helps Dad. No, not as a mechanic. Dad wouldn't let her anywhere near his gear. Dad has Chris to help him, a bloke he employs. But now and then Mum helps in the front office. You need someone there at times because Dad and Chris can't do everything by themselves. Before Chris it was a Sri Lankan dude called Angelo.

And sometimes Dad works on Sundays. To finish some work he has promised to someone, he always says. He likes to keep promises. A good habit, he says. You keep your promises, and others will keep theirs. I don't know if anybody has kept any promises to him except Mum who promised to marry him and did, but when Dad believes something there is no point asking questions about it.

And that morning too, as I was coming down the stairs, I could hear him in the toilet, gurgling, probably getting ready to keep a promise to somebody. The toast was popping in the kitchen. A sure sign Mum was preparing breakfast. If I hadn't been up in ten minutes, she would have gone to the bottom of the stairs and yelled: "Shehaaaaan! Coffee is getting cold." And she hasn't even poured the coffee yet!.

I walked into the kitchen, yawning. The kettle was on and the toast on the plate.

"What time did you get home last night?" Mum asked, in a monotone, putting in four more slices of bread in the toaster. We eat a lot of toast here.

"I dunno, maybe nine, nine thirty."

I guess it must have been around nine thirty. I remember coming in, heating and eating the bowl of pasta left by Mum and going to bed before they got home from their outing. I was so tired I must have fallen asleep straightaway.

"Were you at the station all that time?"

Again, a monotone. I hate this tactic. Questions in monotones make you feel like you are in a courtroom or something. And they always carry the hint of an accusation. How well do you know the defendant? Are you the owner of this vehicle used in the robbery? And when you get it from your own mum, it's worse than getting it from a lawyer or judge.

"yeah."

"With Robbie?"

I kinda knew it was coming. I did not want to mention Robbie, but that's just pointless. My parents know that I hang out with Robbie and the gang. They are ok with it. To a point.

My parents are not what you'd call typical Sri Lankans. Well, I guess I can't really say that because I wouldn't know what a typical Sri Lankan is. Racial profiling, Miss Faith, our English teacher, would hiss if she heard it. But I am only comparing my parents to their Sri Lankan friends, the only other Sri Lankans I know. They are like Mum and Dad only in their houses and their cars. In every other way they are different. Oh I don't mean they are nasty or anything. They are pretty nice. They smile a lot, laugh a lot and joke a lot, even if the jokes are usually pretty lame. They always ask me how I am going in my studies and comment how tall I have grown or something like that. They love to comment on my growth, I swear. If I grow tall the way they keep imagining things I'd soon be hitting the ceiling, I reckon. But they also have this weird thing that they are Sri Lankan, even though they have lived here for I don't know how long. They want their kids to learn Sinhalese, eat curry, go to temples and basically associate with Sri Lankans, even if some of the poor kids were born here. I tell you there is a whole generation of Sri Lankans growing up speaking in Aussie accents and knowing only other Sri Lankans speaking in Aussie accents. And, I am pretty sure they want them to marry Sri Lankans too. But that is nothing compared to what they want from their kids when it comes to studies. An ATAR below 90 is a sin, and anything below 80 would signify some disease or serious mental disorder at worst. Take this girl for instance, Lalani, the daughter of uncle Gamini, one of Dad's good mates. Poor thing, she badly wanted to do fashion design, had her heart set on it. But her mum cried 'No way!' and her dad asked 'are you crazy?' and the poor, frightened kid threw her arms up and said alright, alright I'll do pharmacy! She crammed like hell but got nowhere near enough marks to do pharmacy and ended up doing some course that satisfied neither she nor her parents.

My parents are totally different. I just can't imagine my dad going now, now, Shehan, stop piss-farting around 'cause you're going to be an astronaut! They have this philosophy that is kinda weird but also cool. You are free to do what you like, they say. We can only tell you what is right and wrong, but at the end of the day it is your life. Buddhism, says Dad. So they tell me that smoking is bad for me, drugs will kill me, studying hard is good for me, being nice to people is good for me, learning Sinhalese, maybe good for me because it is part of my heritage, and, of course curry is the best kinda food in the world. But I am free to decide. Only thing they insist on is in telling the truth. No matter what, you can't lie. You either tell the truth or make no comment. And of course, no swearing in front of them.

I don't know how they became like this, but I have heard Dad say that when he wanted to marry Mum, their parents just went spastic for some reason and they had to runaway together and get married against their parents' wishes. Dad's mum died of a heart attack having heard that. I guess that is why he decided that he would never put his own son under pressure. Good for them and good for me too.

And I gotta say it works most of the time. Sure, I don't like curry that much and my Sinhalese is limited to a few polite greetings and many swear words I have picked up from the kids of Mum's and Dad's Sri Lankan friends, but I am also not into any serious shit. Whenever I feel like doing something I know they won't approve of, I don't do it. There is something inside telling me this is gonna end in shit. I never lie to them, just avoid telling the truth if I have to, and I never get in to fights and shit. It's just that we can't stop Gary from Bashing Robbie and Robbie from bashing others.

It was good to have parents like that. Imagine having a bastard like Gary! I have heard my parents say that if you do something bad in this life, it comes back to haunt you in the next. I am not big on religion, but I have to admit that sounds pretty sensible. Assuming that it is also true, I cannot imagine what kinda shit Robbie must have done in his last life and what kinda good I have.

But this doesn't mean that my parents are totally cool with the idea of me hanging out with Robbie. Not that they know that Robbie goes spastic sometimes, that Gary bashes Robbie and that Robbie bashes others. I wonder how the Buddhist philosophy would deal with that if they knew it. But I guess they can kinda sense something when they speak to Robbie, which, mind you, they haven't done on more than a couple of times. Not that Robbie is aggressive in their presence or anything like that. The contrary. He is always polite with them, too fucking polite to tell the truth. So fucking polite that he hardly says anything, and, as a result, Mum and Dad think he is some kind of retard. Well they don't exactly say it, but it is implied, you see. Questions like 'when is he going to speak a sentence?', 'Has he not heard of water?' Imply that they think he is some sort of a weirdo. They can't see why I am hanging out with someone like that, me their only son hanging out with a dude who can barely make conversation with an adult. But they don't stop me from doing that. As Dad says, there are all kinds of people in this world, and we got to live with them. Besides, it's my life. But it is a worry to them. I can see that in their eyes and in the way they speak. Especially in the monotone.

"Are you up to date with your schoolwork?"

"Yup." Monotone responded with a monotone. It's a good tactic if you can keep it up. And the answer is true too. I am always up to date with work, even if I am not getting A's all the time.

"How is Robbie with his studies?"

This time the tone is slightly different. The prosecution is ze-roing in on the accused.

"Alright, I guess."

Not really true. That boy rarely touched a book in his life. Maybe once in a while to swat a fly or something like that, but never really to read or to write in.

"Really?" She knows. Now the tone is sarcastic. The only thing worse than a monotone. From a mum.

"Does he ever go to school?"

I can't help smiling now. Clever Mum. She knows how not to mince words sometimes.

"'Course he does," I say, munching a piece of toast. "What do you think he is? Some kinda retard?"

Mum gives me the look which says it all.

I hear Dad coming out of the bathroom. He is already wear-ing his overalls. Yes. Promises to keep.

"Who's a retard?" He asks, pouring some coffee.

Then he sees me and smiles. "Ah, good morning young man!" He chirps as he sips the coffee. "What time did you leave Robbie last night?"

THREE

When my dad asked what time I left Robbie he was making a point. I was way too attached to Robbie.

Sometimes I have heard people ask the question, if you have only one person to hang out with in the world who would it be? That is a stupid and unfair question, if you ask me. It is stupid because you are never likely to get into a situation where you have to choose just one person to hang out with. Unfair because it makes people choose between all kinds of different people they love equally. But if someone had asked me those days who that one person was I would have had no hesitation in answering. It had to be Robbie. Sorry, Mum and Dad.

Robbie McMillan. Tall, wiry and very, very blond.

About a year ago, when he walked in to our class and into my life I was only just beginning to find some people hot in a way that stirred something inside me, all the way from heart to groin. Well, the groin most of the time. And I was finding boys, tall, athletic and preferably blond boys hotter than curvy, busty girls in tight jeans and short skirts, blond or not. At first, this was not a very comforting feeling, I must admit. I knew there was no law against a guy liking a guy but the law is not everything you see. I have seen how hard it was for Freddie Jameson who was branded a 'fag", simply because he was thought to look like one, pale, thin and girly. He was teased mercilessly until he had to move school, having everything from his lunch box to his school bag stolen and everything from his hair to his heart made a mess of. And I could only admire the guts of little Jessie Nicholson who was gay and so fucking proud of it to the point of telling everyone at school about it and copping all the shit for it without batting an eyelid. I did not want to be like any of them if that was what it took to be a *fag*. Besides I had no idea how my liberal parents would take this despite all their 'it's your life' philosophy. What kind of Buddhist saying my father would pull out of the hat to deal with it, or even whether he would still stick to Buddhism if he suspected his son had faggy feelings.

And the faggy feelings were of a very unusual kind, I gotta say. I got excited by the sight of hot athletic boys, but I had little intention of taking it any further. I didn't even try to get friendly with Jack Landis or Aaron Bathurst, the two hottest jocks at school. I just liked seeing them, feeling my heart racing and my body going numb each time I passed them or saw them play footy on the oval. None of the jocks I liked to perv at were my friends. Well, I didn't really have any friends to start with so I guess having someone like Jason or Jack for friends was wishful thinking, but it was good to dream. And like most dreams, it got nowhere. Hell, those guys didn't even know I existed! I have lost count of the times I tried to smile with Jack only to see him look straight through me. I tell you it's a pity when such a good-looking guy has to be such a prick. But I guess he could afford to ignore a fag like me when there were loads of girls wanting to do more than smile with him all the time. The only real release for my feelings was when I wanked myself to sleep in the night, thinking of Jack's torso bathed in sweat or Aaron's long, muscly legs straining as they ran after the footy. Only the bed sheets knew my feelings.

Maybe I was too scared. Or maybe I wasn't even really sure which way I was heading.

See, when Diane Peterson walked past me at school, swaying her hips under the skirt that was just a tad shorter than regulation length, I got goosebumps and a stirring in my pants. But that was all there was to it. I never bothered to do anything about it. Just watched the hips sway by. But one thing was certain. If I was to have a wank in the night I wouldn't toss a coin to see if it was over Jack or Diane. I just thought of Jack and tossed.

But although I may be a fag, - or half-fag - I do not look like one. I don't look girly at all. Shit, I even had hair on my lips long before anyone else in my grade. And I am not the nerdish sort of guy, I swear. Despite what my dad's friends keep saying, I am not tall, but not skinny and weedy-looking either and I wear no glasses, in my opinion, a pre-requisite for a nerd. I wouldn't say I am good looking but I have my Dad's broad forehead and Mum's classic nose which makes me look kinda attractive without making heads turn. If anything made me faggy or nerdy outwardly it was the fact that I was not the outgoing type. I had very little interest in sport, not even in cricket which Sri Lankans are supposed to be mad about. My interest was unique for a boy. I liked cooking. I don't know exactly when it started but ever since I can remember I have been interested in preparing food. I remember helping Mum in the kitchen as a little kid and then trying my hand at cooking on my own, and I swear to this day I can rustle up a good lunch or dinner, and not just for myself. I have heard some of Dad's and Mum's friends say that it is strange for a boy to be interested in cooking instead of just eating. But my parents aren't worried though. Mum often gets me to help in the kitchen and even to cook although at times I can't help but think that sometimes she is slightly worried. "It's good that you will always be able to look after yourself Shehan", she says, ruffling my hair when I have cooked something nice. "But it would be better if you develop other interests too." Dad simply says do what you like but don't do anything stupid.

So being the mateless Sri Lankan interested in cooks and jocks, I would spend my recess and lunch in the library, browsing through cookery books with an occasional foray into the magazine section to check out the sports mags. They had some hot guys in them. And the library also had these huge windows that opened to the oval and I had a clear view of all the jocks running around playing footy and touch rugby. It was not an ideal situation but it passed the time. Nobody really bothered me much for doing this. I was rarely if ever teased. I guess nobody found anything in me worth teasing about. Or they just didn't give a shit about a weirdo who spent his recess and lunch in the library reading cookery books when he wasn't staring out of the window.

Then, one morning, just before recess, Robbie walked in. It was a Monday, sometime in the spring.

We knew he was coming because there was a rumour going around that a kid who had been expelled from at least ten other schools was to join us. That caused a bit of a stir, even if you allow a bit of exaggeration on the part of the rumour-mongers. There is no way anyone can get expelled from ten schools and still want to go to school.

But we were not surprised that our school took somebody like that in, even though the baddest kid we had, Silvio, had been expelled only from three schools. Ours is a state school. Not a bad one but not a very good one either. It delivers decent VCE results. My dad can afford to send me to a private school. Maybe not Haileybury or Scotch but a decent one; but he decided against it. Kids will learn no matter where they are if they are motivated enough, and if the school had decent teachers, was his motto. You didn't have to pay loads of money to find that out. The fact that the school produced decent VCE results was a sign that it had decent teachers and some kids were motivated enough to do well. Therefore it was my responsibility to find the motivation. If I wasn't motivated enough, well, then that was my problem. Buddhism, Dad's style.

But back to Robbie. Being a half-decent state school that took anyone in, our school accepted him, apparently with the warning that at the first serious misdemeanour he would find himself without a school again. That was a joke. We all knew that. The principal should have said at the first serious misdemeanor the school became aware of – or cared about.

Anyway, they took Robbie in and he walked into our class on a Monday morning, just before recess. Tall, wiry and the absolutely blond hair disheveled, white shirt hanging out, top button undone, showing a patch of strong, smooth chest. A fag's dream. He walked in, gave a note to Mr. Henderson the Math teacher who was struggling to make a particularly boring problem intolerable, and without waiting for Hendo to say anything, walked straight in. A hush fell on the class as we all realized who had walked in. But Hendo wasn't taken aback by the reputation of the boy who had pissed off ten schools. He wanted to stamp is authority at the very beginning. So he asked Robbie to stop and tuck his shirt in.

Robbie did. But in the most outrageous way.

He stopped and turned towards Hendo. Then he unzipped his fly and very dramatically, and deliberately, began to neatly tuck the white shirt in, giving Hendo a full view of his package encased in dark blue undies. He kept tucking the shirt in, taking his time, all the time looking Hendo in the eye. And I swear if Hendo's eyes had opened any bigger they would have popped right out.

And then the final touch.

Just before he finished ticking the shirt in Robbie let the pants drop. He made it appear as if they slipped out of his hands but I am sure he dropped them on purpose. The class roared with laughter as Robbie bent down coolly, picked up his pants and went on doing it all over again.

After a full two minutes of shirt-tucking, he was done. "Happy?" He asked

If Hendo was happy his words failed him.

And so much for serious misdemeanours.

Then the joy of joys: Robbie came and sat next to me.

Well, that was because that was the only seat available and he just made for it and dropping the only book he carried on the desk, plonked himself on the chair. As he did he cast the most cursory glance at me. I had already seen his ass and the stirrings had begun within. The sight of those blue eyes made them a tad violent.

"Hey," he said, cool and casual.

"'ey," I said, dry-throated.

Then the recess bell rang.

By the end of recess, Robbie had punched Silvio in the face.

Not many people saw it. Silvio, it happens, had been bragging about showing Robbie his place ever since he learnt about Robbie coming to our school. Silvio was not really a bully but one of those tough guys who just wanted people to show him respect. People usually did and Silvio didn't bother anyone as long as the respect was there. There was nobody in school who wanted to challenge him. But Robbie was different. With Robbie he really felt that he had a potential challenger. He was keen to nip that challenge in the bud.

And Robbie showed him his place alright.

I saw it happen right in front of my eyes. I had given the library a break that day, too excited by the prospect of having Robbie in class. I followed him around watching him walk out of the class and sitting outside in the sun, blond hair blazing. He wasn't talking to anyone, just sitting there gazing at the oval. He was sizing things up I guess, probably wondering how long he was gonna stay in this school. There were dozens of kids standing around, watching him like some animal on show. Well, he was, I guess. A magnificent animal.

Then, Silvio showed up.

He walked up to Robbie, trying to make it appear causal, swaggering almost. I guess he wanted to show how fearless he was, how cool he was and that Robbie's reputation meant nothing to him. But you could see that he was not sure. Of himself or Robbie, because I swear I saw the legs wobble as they reached Robbie.

We inched closer to see and hear better.

We heard nothing though. Apparently Silvio was saying something to Robbie and Robbie was not paying attention. He was ignoring Silvio. I guess he had seen plenty of Silvio's in the schools he had been kicked out of. But Silvio was not to be ignored. He said something else and then, when Robbie said nothing, he bent down, his face about a foot from Robbie's and pushed Robbie by the shoulder.

A hush went around as Robbie looked up. His face had that look which said, mate, you have just crossed the line.

Silvio said something and pushed him again.

Robbie punched him. Once. In the face.

Silvio reeled. He did not fall but reeled backwards steadying himself on his thick wog legs. A gasp went around the crowd. Several kids jumped to separate the fighters but that was not necessary. There was no fight. Robbie was still sitting there, totally ignoring the drama. Silvio was too busy holding his bleeding nose to retaliate.

By lunch time the news had spread that Silvio had been owned by Robbie. Silvio spent the rest of the day nursing his bloody nose and mouth. He vowed revenge but nobody saw him go anywhere near Robbie after that. As for the teachers they did not know about the incident. They preferred to have it that way. So much for serious misdemeanours.

And by the end of the day, Robbie had little group of disciples. I was one of them.

During the rest of that day in class, he sat next to me. I was in heaven. The jock of the world was sitting right next to me. Sure he stank like hell. I am sure he had not showered for days. But that was a small price to pay to be next to him. I could not help stealing glances at him and each time he said something to me my heart fluttered violently. And those teeth! They were the whitest teeth I have seen. I swear if he did not shower he took good care of his teeth. Either that or he just had naturally stunning teeth, like the rest of him.

We talked a little. It was mostly me helping him out with stuff. English, Math, Chem. He was not dumb (got it Dad?) but totally lost. Like he didn't know some of the basic chem. stuff he should have known in term one and he had no idea how to do a language analysis. I guess if you keep changing schools so often as he is supposed to have done you will be lost. But he was quick to pick up stuff. We were analyzing this article on whaling and I explained to him what a 'contention' was. He got it quickly and wrote that the contention of the article was that the Japs don't give a shit about whales, only their meat. Spot on, although not exactly the wording Miss Faith would have preferred. And 'whales' was spelt without an 'H' and 'meat' was spelt with a double E. But he was trying and I was only too glad to help, even though most of the time my whole body was quivering inside from the excitement of sitting next to him, sometimes even making it difficult to hold the pen properly.

During lunch, I hung out with him near the oval. I was thrilled that I was the only person he showed an interest in speaking to. I could see other kids staring at us, some quite amused to see me, of all people, talking to the bad boy and others clearly envious. Robbie ignored them all and just chatted with me. He even offered me a fag! I refused and said he would get into trouble if smoked right there in front of everybody. Yup, he said and promptly went behind the lab and did it.

While he smoked I learnt a few things about him, like his name, which schools he had been to and what kinda things he liked. Man, he *had* been to a few schools, maybe not ten, but it was getting close to that. He had repeated year 10 once and was now nearly 18. And to my great joy I discovered that he lived not very far from me, actually about15 minutes walking distance even though I had never seen him around town. He lived in a little flat with his mum, dad and little sister and worked some evenings delivering pizzas and sometimes unloading containers for a local company. And he didn't like too many things, playing footy now and then with a local club, catching a movie with his girlfriend. That was about it. I guess smoking was one of his hobbies too but he didn't have to tell me that. By the end of lunch, he had smoked two fags and was going for the third one when the bell rang.

I also got the chance to see him up close. God! He *was* handsome! He looked like a street kid in school uniform but a bloody hot one. The dirt and grime did little to hide the strong chin, high cheekbones, long slender nose, full, red lips and blue eyes thatched with that dancing blond hair. All of that on an athletic frame that was perhaps six foot two or six foot three. Long, strong arms covered with a thin film of golden hair that glistened in the sunlight as he raised them to brush his hair off or to put the fag to his mouth. Hot! I swear if Hitler was alive or if Robbie was in Nazi Germany they would have thrown him under a shower, dressed him in some smart uniform and photographed him for their latest calendar.

Only the eyes seemed sad though. Not downright dripping sad but kinda lost sad. Deep blue eyes searching for something they can't find. But I gotta say it made the face look hotter. For a fag like me at least.

Towards the end of lunch, Marty and Mark joined us. They were two fuckwits at school who had no other friends than themselves. Marty in particular was a pimply, stocky kid who always rolled his sleeve up to display his arms that honestly had more fat than meat. Both thought they were jocks but they were the only people who seemed to think so. I swear they believed they were being up themselves and not giving a shit about anybody when others were simply avoiding them. Apparently they had known Robbie in a previous school. They too had been expelled, but only twice. "Good to have ya here mate," Marty said, slapping him on the back, throwing a questioning glance at me as if to ask what the fuck are you doing here? Retard trying to edge out the closet fag. Obviously they didn't think that I was in Robbie's league.

But Robbie did. Throughout the rest of the lunch he spoke more to me than to those two idiots and after school he waited for me to walk to the station with him. I did, with that quivering still inside me and waited for him to get on the train hoping that the train would be at least a few minutes late.

* * *

Most kids our age hang out at the mall, or the video arcade. But we hung out at the station. It was a normal suburban station I guess, no big deal with two old wooden – some say historic – shelters for waiting passengers and two ticket machines on each platform. A bus stopped right outside the station bringing passengers from other parts of town. On either side were pretty high embankments connecting with the platforms by ramps. The place was hardly crowded, at least not when we were there which was usually in the evening. Only a few people getting in and out and nobody staying on the platform longer than the arrival of the next train. It meant we had the platform to ourselves, more or less, at least that corner of it where the bench stood under the light.

It was a perfect place to hang out if you wanted to be on your own. I guess that is what we wanted. Plus, Robbie had been hanging out there with Sarah before he met us. It was like his favourite place. I remember asking him once why he liked the station so much. He said it was because of the trains. It made him feel that if he ever got bored he could always hop on a train and go somewhere, north or south. And sometimes in the evening he even walked home along the tracks, walking until they crossed the street and then walked up the street to his home.

Sarah was a weird girl. Dark blond, medium height and slightly on the plump side. She had more boobs than brains, Marty was fond of saying when she and Robbie were not around. She was attractive. True, she came to see Robbie heavily made up but that did not make her look sluttish. Underneath the heavy paint, there was something of a natural prettiness which she was unfortunately trying to muck up with her make-up, though not with much success. And she was quite nice too, except when she babbled continuously. She lived somewhere close to the city with her dad and step mum who, it appeared, only noticed her when she turned up for meals. At other times she would be robbing the bank down the street and they wouldn't know. And they didn't care.

And she was crazy! She would come on the train from the city and get off on the opposite platform, then dart across the tracks and scramble up our side of the platform, sometimes still in her school uniform. And sometimes she would do it with Robbie when they were leaving, frequently when the train was approaching. But somehow it didn't seem so dangerous when Robbie was with her. His long legs took him across easily and he always had his strong arm around Sarah's waist.

Usually, we met there at around five. Not every day but most days. On that first day at school, Robbie had casually mentioned that he usually hung out at the station with his girlfriend and that we were welcome to join him if we did nothing in the evening. Naturally, I was only too glad to oblige and when we went there in the evening I found that Marty and Mark had also taken him up on the invitation. Thereafter we met there regularly. At first, I wasn't sure if Robbie really wanted us to be there but he never said anything. I guess he was glad for the company. He could always meet Sarah on his own if he wanted to and sometimes they would leave early, get on the train and go god knows where. Besides, I figured that he must sometimes get tired of Sarah's company. I know we did.

Of course, Robbie would decide when we met. He had been given that authority without any contest. And I would go home, grab something to eat, then race to the station. Usually, Robbie would be there, sitting on the bench in the far corner, back against the lamp post. If Sarah was already there she would be leaning against his knees, or between them with Robbie's long arms around her. Often Marty and Mark will be there too. But by six all of us would be there, sitting around, talking crap, Robbie and Marty smoking, Sarah occasionally stealing a puff from Robbie's fag.

To somebody seeing us there, we would have looked like a bunch of street kids, homeless and nowhere to go. It was not a totally wrong picture though. I guess we were all misfits, in different ways. Robbie the kid from a violent home, Sarah another troubled kid from a home that just didn't give a crap, me, a closet fag without mates, and Marty and Mark, two wannabe jocks who could not find anybody to admire them. It was a perfect example of birds of a feather flocking together.

Gradually Marty and Mark also warmed to me. I guess they realized that Robbie was cool with me and they could not shake me off. So they treated me with some consideration but with a certain coldness attached to it. I could live with that, as long as I could be with Robbie.

By the start of that summer, we had morphed into a tight unit. We were not super close, but were becoming more and more comfortable with each other, comfortable enough to do things together other than just sit around and talk crap. Sometimes we walked to the mall and had maccas or watched a movie. Occasionally we did go to the park down the road and kick the footy around a bit. I was hopeless at it and often Robbie would laugh hysterically at my lack of co-ordination and ruffle my hair playfully when I missed a kick, which made me even deliberately miss the ball to invite that affectionate touch. But after a few attempts at chasing the ball or kicking it I would tire and sit on the park bench with Sarah and just watch Robbie and the others, but mostly Robbie, kicking and chasing the ball.

I think Robbie came to enjoy having us around him. This was probably the first time he had a group of people around him. He didn't say so exactly but I gathered from what he had told me now and then that until he met us he had had few mates, at least few mates he could hang out with. Maybe he put others off with his temper or maybe he just couldn't find the kind of misfits who wanted to spend their evenings at the station with him and Sarah. Whatever it was, I could see that he liked being with us. On the first day, he had just casually asked us to join him without expecting us to. It was like, 'if you guys wanna come fine but if not no worries'. But when we became a regular fixture he would basically order us to be there when he was there because now he had begun to like it. As much as the company, I am sure he also enjoyed the respect and attention he got from us. He was the unquestioned leader, the guy who made the decisions.

You could see it in his behaviour, in his body language. He was a lot more relaxed and talkative unlike at school where he usually kept to himself. That is when he was at school which was like only every other day. But when he was at school – where, to my great joy he always sat next to me - he spent a lot of time daydreaming or drawing funny faces in his books. He was good at it too, I must say. He could draw Mr. Serbovic exactly like him though in a funny way and his portrait of Miss Faith wasn't too bad either. In everything else, I had to help him though. So lost was he. And apart from me, Marty and Mark, his buddies from the station, he spoke to very few people, not even the girls. Many of the girls who had drooled over him at first soon lost interest in him simply because of that. They probably concluded that he was too weird, maybe even too cocky. Robbie did play a bit of footy during recess and lunch but showed little interest in socializing with other jocks. And the jocks kept him at a distance, though they were outwardly friendly. I guess although they realized he was no big challenge to them where the chicks were concerned, they also didn't want to get on his wrong side.

I think Robbie found the whole school experience a bit too much and felt out of place in that environment. School was not a place where he felt at home. If anything it made him uncomfortable. You could see from the way he kept to himself and struggled his way through most conversations as if he did not know what to say. If Mum and Dad had seen him at school they would have been totally convinced that he was, after all, a social retard. But staying away from people did not keep Robbie away from trouble. But that, I gotta say, was not something he could avoid because Silvio is not the only practising idiot in our school. A few of them wanted to test if they could succeed where Silvio didn't. A broken tooth here, a black eye there and a lot of pain everywhere soon convinced them that Silvio's bloody nose was no fluke. That didn't win Robbie any friends though. Kids feared him and respected him but they didn't love him. We were the only people who really warmed to him.

That is why I think he felt very much at home with us at the station. He laughed a lot, talked a lot and was generally a lot more relaxed than at school. You could even say he was happy, sitting on the bench, hugging Sarah who snuggled up to him and chatting with us about anything that fancied him at the time and we would listen to him and follow him, eagerly. At home he was getting into trouble and at school he was trying to stay out of trouble, but at the station, with us, he was always in command.

Sarah did not mind us being at the station at all. I guess to her it made things a bit more interesting. She was nice to us but she never treated us as any more or less than Robbie's friends. She could be asking me how I was and the next moment she'd be turning around and biting Robbie's lip or something without showing the slightest interest in my response. I can't really complain though. I was equally distracted by Robbie. Sometimes when I sat on the bench at the park watching Robbie and the guys kick the footy she would talk to me about all kinds of things, about herself, about her school, about the supermarket where she worked as a checkout chick but usually, I heard little as I paid more attention to Robbie running around in the park than to her sitting right next to me and yapping on about things that I couldn't care less about. She didn't seem to mind though.

For me, however, the whole experience was a dream come true. I have been dreaming of being the friend of a jock for so long and now I was sitting around with one, and one of the hottest jocks at that. I would sit there simply thrilled by his presence, listening to him, watching the blond hair bounce and wave as he turned, the thick lips part to bare those dazzling teeth and watching those long, strong arms snaking around Sarah and hugging her to him. It made me feel a tad jealous of Sarah but strangely it was not a kind of hostile jealousy. Not even envy but a sad feeling that I did not have that pleasure or privilege.

The only person who spoiled the fun was Gary, with his fits

of temper. According to Marty, he worked for a demolition company. I did not know that he tried his profession on his poor son until Robbie turned up a couple of times with a bruised face and teary eyes. I wondered if he had been in a fight but it seemed strange that Robbie could be beaten by someone so badly. But I had no idea that he had been beaten by the one person who could have done that – his dad. Of course ,Sarah and even Marty and Mark knew that, they had known Robbie longer than I had, and one day when Robbie and Sarah were getting delayed Marty told me the whole story. Gary was a bastard who went spastic now and then for nothing. He usually tried to bash Robbie's mum and Robbie had to intervene. And then Robbie got bashed. Never too violently but enough to bruise his face and make him cry. "He just likes to see me cry", Robbie said the next time he came with bruises and tears.

It was truly sad to see Robbie reduced to that. The big, blond stud sitting on the bench, sniffling and sobbing. Sarah would make a wifely attempt to console him, hugging him and kissing him while we sat around, sad and helpless. I guess I was hurting more than Sarah, Marty or Mark, wanting so badly to hold him and unable to do so.

And after the tears, anger would erupt and Robbie would go spastic. Not all the time, but often. Once he picked a fight with a guy at the station who was staring at his bruises and would have punched him if we hadn't held him. At another time some idiot at work asked him if he had been punched by his girlfriend and Robbie punched him to show he was not. He got fired but Robbie didn't care. He had got his anger out. But I gotta say this for Robbie. He bashed people but only when provoked, even if it did not take much to provoke him when he was in that mood.

And there was nothing we could do to stop it. Marty and

Mark were never going to utter a word to stop him and neither was I. We were terrified when he was in a rage and when he cooled down we all thought it was over. Not that Robbie would have listened to any of us anyway. Only Sarah said anything to him and she simply threw fits and the way Robbie yelled back at her showed us all how stupid it would be to think that we could change him.

Once, just once, the school took an interest in Robbie's case. We had this new counsellor who was trying to make a good impression on the management. So, having heard about Robbie's anger issues but not about the issues behind the anger, he set an appointment with Robbie and tried his best anger management strategies on Robbie. The session did not last more than five minutes. Robbie stormed out of the counsellor's little hidey-ho after telling him that he had better things to do than speak to some fag who had no idea what he was talking about. I guess he was right. The counsellor, Mr. Wilmot, seemed to live in his own little world. When he met kids in the schoolyard he would speak to them as if they were primary kids, even if the kids were in year 12 and had more hair on their cheeks than he did. That is probably how he spoke to Robbie too. It's a miracle he didn't get a taste of Robbie's anger. I am sure he was well qualified, just not too good at his job. At least not good at dealing with the violence in kids like Robbie.

But violence - and smoking - I gotta say, were like Robbie's only real vices. Unlike most boys of his age from that kind of background, he did not drink, ever. Marty and Mark often bragged about downing a six pack or a few vodkas at a party but we never saw them do that. Robbie simply said he didn't like that shit. And he did not take drugs or break into houses to support that habit. He was a good kid. Violent, yes, but good. Even the violence he could do little to control. I guess Gary controlled it most of the time.

I have seen Gary only once. One day we were at the mall, returning from a movie, Robbie and Sarah had gone to get some fags and we were waiting for them. Suddenly Marty nudged me in the ribs and pointed to someone near the Safeway. There was a man, huge, with bushy hair and beard, with a little blonde woman and a little girl. That was Gary, Marty whispered. There at the mall, he looked huge but normal, almost like a kind and fatherly bear as he gave a lolly to little Megan. But I could just imagine the nastiness in that body and the violence it could arouse.

It was also easy to see where Robbie got his looks from. Hair and face from the mother. Build from the father. And Gary I am sure gave him the temper too. The sad, lonely nature he probably got from his little blonde mother who looked sad even while standing there outside the shops.

One day I asked Robbie if Gary was ever nice to him. Maybe when I was little, he said. But he could not remember that far back.

But if Gary insisted on spoiling our party we were determined to have fun despite him. That summer was particularly magical. I was so glad that we were not going to Sri Lanka that year. We went every other summer and this was the one where we stayed in Melbourne. Not that I didn't like going to Sri Lanka. It was fun, cool without being really awesome, at least for the first week when you are just getting used to the dust and the heat, the noise and the crowds. Everybody is new, even though you met them all two years ago. Then the dust becomes dust, the heat becomes the heat and everybody except Mum and Dad become boring and tedious, asking the same questions over and over again. Time to get back with some good memories and loads of pirate DVDs. Something I wouldn't mind doing, but not when I had Robbie.

So that summer, without an overseas trip to interfere, I spent hours with Robbie and the gang. It never made me tired or bored. Being with Robbie was something I could do for hours, even days. But we also did other things. Going to movies, the maccas and stuff like that. Sometimes when we went out, Robbie brought little Megan with him. She was tiny and cheeky. She loved being with her big brother who treated her like a little princess. Robbie bought her anything as long as he could afford it and even carried her around sometimes on his back even though she was nearly seven. Megan loved it. I guess she could see the whole world from the shoulders of her tall, big brother. Once we even went to the MCG to see Australia play some foreign team, all of us wrapped in Aussie flags. Robbie came in his thongs and shorts and nothing else and I walked around the stadium, like in a dream, proud to be seen with this magnificent stud. We hung around in the old Bay Thirteen and Robbie got into a fight with a bloke who spilled a beer all over him. Robbie landed a good punch but ended up copping more beer from the dude's mates. All of us got thrown out and we went straight from the grounds to our station where we sat wrapped in our flags, laughing about the stupid fight. Movies were fun too. Almost every time we were at the movies Marty farted, not loudly but really stinky little farts that made everyone know he had farted merely by the smell. It caused Sarah to giggle uncontrollably and Robbie to be in stitches. Once we all had to leave because Robbie couldn't take it anymore. He laughed and laughed until he got up and walked out, still laughing, people in the audience shooing him. Naturally, we followed him. Occasionally I got the chance to sit next to him. It was not often as

Sarah would sit with him on one side and Marty or Mark would grab the seat on the other side. But sometimes I won the race and spent the movie feeling myself going all warm and wriggly inside. By now I had got so used to his smell that it did not even register. Only his presence mattered.

Sometimes we did strange things. Once on a Saturday almost on a whim we got on the train and went all the way to Ballarat. We took Megan along. We bummed around the town, having lunch at KFC and in the afternoon just walked around the countryside, Robbie carrying Megan on his back. The little kid was so happy, carried by her big brother, and treated like royalty by everybody. We swam in some creek, Robbie tried to get on a horse in a paddock and got nearly kicked by it and all of us got chased by a big fucking dog when Marty tried to steal some tomatoes from a farm, Robbie running with Megan on his back, Megan laughing as if it was the funniest thing she had seen even though we were scared shitless. We returned in the evening, tired but happy.

Did Robbie ever suspect that I had a crush on him? It was hard to say. A few times he had caught me staring at him and our eyes had met and he had looked away, as if he felt awkward. Uneasy. Once I remember I asked him how tall he was and he just stood before me, like a giant, and holding me by the shoulders looked down on me, in this fake bullying pose, strong hands grasping my shoulders. "I don't know", he hissed through his teeth, trying to sound mean. "But I am fucking head and shoulders above you!" It was true. He was above me, not just physically. I looked up and our eyes met for a split second and he suddenly let go, as if he had seen something that unsettled him. And when I gave him a present for his birthday he was very confused. The present was this steel bracelet which I thought would look really studly on him. I told him I had got it from one of Dad's friends when in truth I had bought it with the pocket money I had saved. It was a real faggy thing to do I guess, giving Robbie that bracelet. He was truly stumped. I guess it was the first time he had ever got a present from a friend – his mum gave him presents and little Megan he said always drew a picture for him. And of course, Sarah gave him stuff. But friends never gave him anything. I guess he had had no real friends for that, only people that hung out with him. But still, it made him look really unsure, maybe even worried.

But he took it, mumbled a thanks, and to my great joy, put it on. It did not matter to me that he told others, especially Sarah who was very curious, that he bought it himself, avoiding my eyes when he said it. I even thought that was better than saying I gave it to him. It would have made things a bit awkward for me too.

Sometimes Marty and Mark would talk about girls, the ones they had fooled around with at a party and the ones they'd like to do it with. I would just sit there wishing the subject would change. Sometimes I would change the subject myself, not having girlfriends to talk about and feeling bloody awkward about it. But sometimes Mark or Marty would ask me, very casually but tongue in cheek of course, about my experiences with the opposite sex. I would lie, saying that I have had a few girlfriends but nothing special. Those two idiots would laugh in a way that showed they knew it was a downright lie. I don't reckon they suspected that I was a fag but I guess they thought I was just a loser just not capable of getting a girl. But fortunately, it would not go any further. It was so fucking ironic because I had never seen those two idiots with any girls but I didn't have the guts to say it. As for Robbie, he would just sit there, hugging Sarah but saying nothing. Sometimes I would glance at him, embarrassed by the talk, wondering what he must be making of the whole conversation only to find him turning his eyes away from mine.

Still, there was one thing that was very noticeable in his attitude to me. He had certain expectations of me, unlike Marty and Mark. He would often tell - almost order -Marty and Mark to make sure they were there at the station the next time we met but he would never tell me. It seemed that it was taken for granted that I would be there with him. Always. And when we went to movies he would naturally choose the movie but he would always ask me if it was ok. He never asked anybody else. Not even Sarah. And he didn't always ask verbally. Sometimes he would just look at me and I would immediately see that he wanted to know. And sometimes I didn't have to say anything. He would see it in my eyes that I was happy to go anywhere he asked. But he always checked. It filled my little budding fag heart with pride to know that Robbie, my idol and my hero, recognized my devotion, and cared for my opinion, in his own way.

And I was always there with him. Every day we met. Even if the others couldn't make it for some reason.

What did I expect from Robbie? It was hard to say as I never really gave it any thought when I was with him. I was just happy that I was with him and I was quite content to relieve my hard-on when I got home, the thought of Robbie's face thatched with that blond hair giving plenty of inspiration for swift relief. Jack and Aaron now did not even get a look in. But beyond that, there were no plans, no hopes. The future was unchartered territory I did not want to explore; the present was a magical country I wanted to live in forever. It didn't really matter to me that he had Sarah, that it was Sarah that he kissed, hugged and smooched all over. I gotta say again, it did make me a tad jealous and hurt to see them there on the bench, Robbie's long arms around Sarah, lips all over her neck, sometimes nibbling her earlobes, her fingers playing with the hair on his arms or the bracelet I had given. At movies, on the odd occasion I got to sit next to him I could see him kissing Sarah passionately and sometimes glimpsed his hand somewhere between her legs. I would try hard to concentrate on the movie, feeling my arousal straining in my jeans. Sometimes I wished it was me, not Sarah. The most I got from him was a firm handshake or an occasional playful headlock if I said something cheeky. But I soon learnt not to think about it. It was easier to enjoy just being with Robbie than longing for a hug. I could always relieve myself at night, alone, in the dark.

* * *

My parents noticed the change in me at a very early stage. From being a kid who seemed to have no friends apart from pots and pans and the computer, I had suddenly turned into Mr. Society, running off to hang out with "friends" almost every evening. Naturally they were pleased to know that I now had friends but they were curious as to who they were, especially when I was usually staring at the TV screen without much interaction during those evenings when Robbie was working and nobody was at the station. Having been teenagers themselves it did not take them long to guess what was going on and my dad – always the smartass – did not mince his words.

"So?" he asked one evening, plonking himself down beside me on the sofa and slapping my thigh. "Who is she?"

I was glad dark skinned people do not blush. Had my skin been paler I would have turned redder than a red light district.

And Dad was right on the money. "Wish you were a bit paler," he said. "It would have been something to behold."

I grinned. But inside I was in turmoil. Obviously Dad had guessed that I was having a crush on somebody. But what would he think if he knew that I had that crush on a guy?

"So who is she?"

I glanced up. There was Mum in the kitchen, ears cocked.

My first impulse was to lie. But that would have broken the non-lying pact.

"No comment."

It was now Dad's turn to grin.

"Alright," he said. "But make sure you don't do anything stupid."

A typically cryptic advice. "Stupid" could have meant anything – getting somebody pregnant, running away from home, neglecting studies or all of the above.

"No I won't," I said. I smiled inwardly imagining getting Robbie pregnant. Boy! That would be something!!

Thereafter Mum and Dad left me alone. No further questions were asked about who I had a crush on. They obviously thought they had done their bit. The rest was up to me.

But their curiosity about my new friends refused to go away. Or to be precise, not allowed to go away. One day one of Dad's friends who had seen us on the railway platform called Dad and bitched about me smoking. It was a mean and petty thing to do because I never smoked and did not have the intention to start. And to Robbie's credit, he never offered me a fag after that first day in school. But this dude tells Dad that I was smoking. I swear some of these guys have nothing better to do than mind other people's business. But all that Dad asked him was whether he actually saw me smoke. No, the nosey friend said, but he was with kids who were smoking. And then a rhetorical question: do you expect me to believe that Shehan would be with such kids and not smoke?

Dad's response was simple: I will ask him. And he did. Right then and there.

"Shehan, do you smoke?"

"Nope."

"Have you ever smoked?"

"Nah. Never."

"Fine."

That was the end of the conversation. But Dad did want to know who the smoking friends were.

I told him, playing down Robbie's background a bit so as not to alarm him. I wasn't breaking the pact about lying. Just avoiding the whole truth.

"Hmmmmm," Dad said. "An interesting crowd." Then he exchanged that 'what do you reckon?' look with Mum. I swear they have this weird way of communicating with their eyes. I guess they have been married for so long that they only have to look at each other to know what they think. It's usually Dad looking at Mum for approval and Mum giving him one of her looks which could mean one of several things. It could be 'Oh ,yes! I totally agree', 'maybe, but I have my , or 'You must be joking!' Today the look was the totally agreeing kind. They don't realise that I have been around long enough to know.

But then an ambush!

"Why don't you invite them here for a barbecue? Your birthday is next Saturday. Call them over." And Mum gives him the total agreement.

But I almost gasped. Call Robbie and the gang? Here? For a barbecue?

I was at once thrilled and scared. Thrilled because I could invite Robbie to my house. Scared because of what Mum and Dad might think of them. I wasn't too worried about them discovering my crush. My straight parents were not equipped with the skills to detect a fag's crush I thought. I was more worried about what they might think of Robbie, seeing him in his dirty jeans and sneakers and smelling him before they could see him, none of which I guessed Robbie would change simply because he was coming to a barbecue at my home. I could even guess what he would say if someone dared to suggest that he dressed differently. "It's a fucking barbecue for fuck's sake!" And I wasn't going to dare and spoil his mood.

And I was spot on. They all came in their glorious grimy best, jeans, sweaty t-shirts, and dirty sneakers. And Robbie in a singlet! Any other time I wouldn't have complained. He looked every inch the stud he was, pecs straining, arms fully exposed. Hot! But not today Robbie!!!

Sarah alone came dressed for the occasion, a nice summer frock and a dainty little handbag. They also brought me a present. A cute little soft toy monkey which Sarah had picked at some shop in the mall. "We thought we'd bring you a friend," she said giggling in her own batty way as she gave it me. "You gotta look after it like a bro," Robbie said, grabbing the monkey and rubbing it playfully in my face.

My parents received them warmly, Dad shaking everybody's hand several times and Mum giving them little pecks on their cheeks. If they were taken aback by the appearance of my friends they did not show it. "So glad you could come," Mum said several times but I could see her eyes roaming all over Robbie and then over Sarah. She must have found it hard to give Robbie that little kiss and Robbie must have felt extremely awkward getting kissed. He simply grunted something, smiling uncertainly.

The barbecue was a quiet affair. And a boring one too. We sat in the backyard under the shade cloth and I was naturally the chef, cooking steaks, lamb and pork chops and sausages. Dad had a couple of beers and tried to engage the visitors in conversation. Only Sarah showed some enthusiasm for that. Not that the others were rude but they were not the kind of people used to making conversation with adults apart from saying 'yeah' and 'nah,' even that only occasionally. After a few futile attempts Dad and Mum retreated to the patio where they sat and watched.

After the barbecue, we sat around and talked, or tried to because everyone seemed to be feeling awkward. This was not our normal haunt. Robbie seemed to be the most uncomfortable, fidgeting and shifting uneasily and not saying much. I was glad he had not smoked but I could say he was controlling the urge with the greatest difficulty. Under the patio, Dad was nodding off. Mum was nowhere to be seen.

BORING!!

Then I had an idea. As usual I had been eyeing Robbie most of that afternoon, taking extra care to pass him the food and drinks. Now, with the conversation drying up I had nothing to do but look at him, and I realized how scruffy he really looked, more than I had ever noticed. Man! He did have something against water! That handsome face was truly patched up with dirt. The hands were dirty too. Dirty and greasy, fingernails blackened as if the fingers had never been dipped in water. True, to me it did not matter, he was as hot as ever. But I suddenly had this urge to play a prank on him, to see how he would look if he washed himself properly, at least a little bit. And as he was not likely to do it himself I would do it for him.

I would have never done anything like that anywhere else but I guess being at home made me bolder. "When was the last time you had a shower?" I asked cheekily and Robbie looked at me surprised. I had never asked him anything like that. And then the inevitable response:

"None of your fucking business!"

There was no anger there. A little bit of embarrassment maybe. But it made him look even hotter, the colour flowing into his cheeks.

And it made me even bolder.

I picked up the garden hose lying on the grass and turned the tap on. "Here," I said. "Let me wash you!"

I turned the water on him.

The water hit Robbie, first soaking his singlet and then splashing his face. I kept the weak spurt on his face, watching the water wet the cheeks, the nose, the chin. God, it was hot!

Robbie was totally surprised. He stood there as if unable to figure out what was going on. The face tightened as anger welled inside.

Others were laughing, Sarah most of all. "Good on ya She-han!" She screamed in delight. "He needed that!"

I watched as Robbie's anger mounted with the laughter, the face red and glowing like it was gonna burst or something. Then suddenly his expression changed as he realized the funny side of it. The lips curved up in a smile and those white teeth flashed. I melted.

Then he was chasing me around the garden and in seconds had me pinned to the ground. We wrestled, or he held me in a gentle headlock and I made a feeble attempt to resist. One long strong arm around my neck, the other pinning my arm to the back, his hair in my eyes and his face pressing on my cheek, his breath full of sweat, onions, lamb chops and a thousand other intoxicating things. Raw. Powerful. Fucking awesome.

Everybody was laughing. Everybody except my parents. From the corner of my eyes, I could see my Dad standing under the patio, a beer in hand looking at us and Mum inside the kitchen looking through the window. In that split second, my eyes met Dad's and I realized he knew. He was probably watching us all afternoon, watching how I gazed at Robbie and how I fussed around him. Now he watched as Robbie held me on the lawn, my face flushed with the ecstasy of his closeness. The look said everything. Yes, my son is a fag.

But nothing was said about it, ever. I guess Dad thought that his initial 'don't do anything silly' caution covered everything.

Also, I guess if my parents were worried about it they also decided that it was best left undiscussed. I never got to find out what they thought about it. Did they think it was a terrible thing? A disorder as I am told many people in South Asian countries believed it to be? Or did they simply think that it was something natural that people experienced? Or was it just a phase people passed through on their way to becoming adults? Knowing my parents I liked to think it was the second one. But I never found out. Maybe I never will.

But they were concerned about Robbie in a different way. They were concerned that he would be a bad influence on me, not where my sexuality was concerned but in other ways. Not knowing Robbie's violence they guessed it, having observed him closely. I don't know how they did it but I guess parents have a way of understanding children. At least some parents do.

"What sort of family does he have?" Dad asked pretty casually, while wiping the dishes that night.

"Mmmmmm..."

"Doesn't look like a boy with a healthy upbringing."

"Well," I said. "His dad is a bit of an asshole"

"Aha!" said Dad. "And the boy is not?"

"No!" I said firmly. "He is a nice kid. One of the nicest!"

Dad quickly realized his mistake. It is silly to try and stand between a boy and his hero.

"I am sure there is a sweet boy underneath all that dirt and grime," Mum said, putting away the plates. "Turning the hose on him was a good idea. A bit extreme but thoughtful."

"The wrestling was interesting too," Dad said, glancing at Mum. "Crude but interesting."

Once again, I was grateful for my dark skin.

FOUR

That Sunday evening, the day after Robbie bashed the Arab, we were in the news.

It did come as a surprise to me. During the early days when Robbie bashed people, I had been on pins for several days worried sick about the consequences. I expected the cops to knock on our door any moment asking for me. But the knock never came. The bashings were not even reported in the media. I guess there were too many of them and too little TV time to bother with them.

So I was relaxed that evening, sitting in the lounge, sipping tea with Dad, watching the evening news. Robbie had said he was not meeting us today. He was taking his mum and Megan to the movies. It was going to be a lazy evening, with only some boring homework and television to occupy myself with and to fill the emptiness I felt from not being able to meet Robbie. Next to me sat Dad, multi-tasking, flicking through a car magazine while following the news.

Then, the newsreader dropped the bombshell.

A vicious racial attack had taken place on a suburban train on

Saturday night, the girl announced, her pretty lips pronouncing 'vicious' and 'racial' as if she was munching something sweet. A gang of at least four, including a girl was involved, she said, mentioning that they all seemed to be young teenagers. Obviously the little girl was too little or too shocked or a bit of both to figure out how old we really were. The leader of the gang, the newsreader said, was a tall blond boy, wearing a dark hoodie and jeans.

Then they showed a picture of the guy, the leader, presumably drawn by a police artist using the description given by the little girl. And of course, she was way off the mark. If the guy in the picture resembled Robbie it was only in his hair. The rest of the face bore no resemblance to him at all. They had made my Robbie look like a thug with blond hair. Well, that kid was scared shitless. You can't expect her to remember anything, really.

I was beginning to feel slightly relaxed when Dad had to spoil it.

"Hey!" He said looking up from his magazine. "That guy looks a lot like your Robbie!"

If I was startled I did my best not to show it. Does he really believe it? If so, boy, we were in deep shit!

I turned my head ever so slightly to look at Dad, with my best, 'yeah right pull the other one Dad' look, hoping that he would not see through it to the panic beneath. But I was worrying unnecessarily. There sat Dad with the biggest grin on his lips. He was kidding. The smartass!

My relief was almost audible.

The news report continued. Now they were showing the injured Arab. Man! These news guys love blood and gore. They show you all kinds of disturbing stuff and before that, they warn you that it's gonna be distressing, as if to cover themselves from distressing us. This report was no different. They were showing close-ups of the man's face all the time warning viewers that some scenes may be distressing to them. And I must admit that it was distressing. Robbie had done a thorough job on the poor bastard as he usually did on people he bashed. His face was covered in bruises and swollen so much it looked like it was about to burst. No wonder he was in the intensive care unit.

But they had got it totally wrong too. Robbie bashed him because he was angry and he was angry because Gary bashed him. The Arab dude's race did not come into the picture at all. I guess Robbie couldn't tell an Arab from a Sri Lankan. He didn't care either. If Gary did not treat Robbie like a punching bag Robbie wouldn't have pummeled that bloke, Arab or not. To call it a racial attack was nonsense. But I guess the newsreader couldn't care less. Maybe she wished it was racial.

"Poor bastard," Dad was saying. He had abandoned the magazine now, eyes fixed on the TV screen.

The man was an Afghan, only recently arrived in Australia. "Welcome to Australia!" Dad said, sadly.

The little girl now appeared on the screen, with several men and women. They were members of the family and the Afghan community. Evidently, the kid was still in shock, hiding behind the dress of a woman who looked like her mum.

"I hope they catch those idiots who did it," Dad said, returning to the magazine.

"Too right!" I agreed. "They should bring back capital punishment."

Of course, I did not mean that. I mean, how can I want my Robbie to be fried in an electric chair? Or get a lethal injection? But I must say I felt sorry for that poor Afghan dude and his little girl. What suffering! For no fault of their own.

We watched the rest of the news in silence. Actually Dad went back to multi-tasking and I just stared at the TV screen. I hardly remembered any of the other news, except that there was something about a labour dispute and the weather guy was going through his boring synoptic chart routine. Then as Dad turned the channel to SBS and went for a toilet break before World News started, I got up and sneaked upstairs to call Robbie.

* * *

When I called Robbie he was in fits. He had seen the news. But then, so had Gary.

And unlike my dad Gary had identified Robbie straightway. Or maybe he just guessed it. Maybe he just wanted to believe it was Robbie because he was spoiling for a fight.

And that is what happened. A fight. And as usual, Robbie came off second-best.

He was crying, saying he just didn't wanna take it anymore. "I don't wanna fucking live here anymore," he was saying." "I am getting outta here." I knew from his tone that he meant it.

"Where would you go?" I asked, my voice quivering. Suddenly I felt more helpless than I had ever been. First, we were all over the news and now Robbie falling apart. Not a nice thing to see or hear.

"Dunno." He said. "I fucking dunno."

It is so sad when Robbie is reduced to this state. I swear. My hero, my beautiful, strong Robbie reduced to a whimpering little boy by his gorilla of a dad. And this time, he seems to have reached breaking point.

"Well, don't do anything silly," I said. I Sounded like Dad, I guess, but that was the only thing I could think of.

"What the fuck do you think I should do now?" He was getting angry now.

"Let me think of something," I said. 'Please."

"Well," he said. "Think fast!"

He hung up. I thought fast. Robbie going spastic again; this time wanting to leave home. What will he do now? Where will he go? Who will he bash? What the fuck can I do about any of this?

But the more I thought the blanker my mind went.

Maybe it was because I was trying to think with my head.

It was only after I started thinking with my heart that I got an idea. And what a brilliant idea it was!!!

Why not get Robbie to move in here? There is a spare room, actually two of them, he can sleep there and go to work and school and do whatever else he wishes. And he can go to school with me! In the evening we can meet at the station as usual. That way I had Robbie with me and my parents didn't have to worry about me coming home late. What a fucking brilliant idea!

I must admit that it was a very simplistic plan. But then as I said I was thinking with my heart. And thinking that was the easy part. I still had to get my parents' approval.

My parents are usually very generous. They do the easy things like giving tax-deductible money to charity but they also do the hard stuff, like Dad giving his old Datsun to one of his mates who had just turned up from Sri Lanka and was looking for a cheap vehicle. Dad gave it as cheap as possible – free. When Dad found that Angelo who used to help him those days had nowhere permanent to live, he turned the little room at the back of the garage which he had been using as a store room into a self-contained joint, complete with a little toilet and shower combination. Alright, he got most of the stuff for the place from somebody who was throwing them away and the guy who set it up gave him a good deal because Dad had done wonders with his car, but still, it was more than anybody would do for a worker. And Dad didn't charge Angelo a cent for the room. When the Tsunami hit he gathered all his spare clothes except for a few shirts and pants and gave them to some dude who was collecting stuff. He was not just helping Sri Lankans either. When the drought was biting hard we drove all the way to some fried-up country town up north with a heap of clothes and toys all packed into a van Dad hired. You should have seen the look on those people's faces! They never expected a black family like ours to visit them - with aid.

Helping other people is a good way to make your own life worthwhile, Dad says. Besides, it's like an insurance policy. If you are nice to people, they will be nice to you. If not in this life, then in the next.

Yes, that was my dad. The philanthropic and philosophical kind. But would he help Robbie? Well, why not? How could my parents turn down the opportunity to help a poor kid in trouble, I thought, even if it was Robbie, the dirty retarded boy on whom their son had a crush. Even if it meant keeping him in their home, at least for a few days. I was sure that to them, tolerating Robbie's unhygienic habits or my little crush on him would be less of an issue than saving him from Gary. At least so I hoped.

Of course, there was the matter of Robbie bashing the Afghan but Dad and Mum didn't really have to know about that, did they?

* * *

But when it came to the issue I found that I had overestimated my parents' philanthropy.

"Are you crazy?" My mother asked. No monotone this time.

"Maybe not completely, but getting there alright," my father, the master of sarcasm.

"What's wrong with Robbie staying with us?" Me, hurt, indignant and steadily going spastic.

"You can't expect us to keep him here?"

"Why not?" I asked, now fast realizing that I was losing the argument and annoyed that my idea was not so brilliant after all, that I had overestimated my parents' goodness.

"I am sure he gets abused as you say. But that doesn't mean that we can keep him here."

Dad sounded dismissive.

"We are not his parents, if he is really in danger there are people he can speak to."

"Like the cops you mean?"

Dad nodded. Mum followed.

I stared at them in disbelief. This is the problem with parents, I swear. They can be the best parents in the whole world but sometimes they think things are so fucking neat and tidy. You get bashed by your dad? Fine! Go tell the cops! Dad doesn't get it, that Robbie is a kid. Eighteen yes, but still a kid in many ways. A lost kid if you ask me. Adults go to the cops. Kids run away. Or worse.

Besides, if Robbie goes to the cops now, not only will they take Gary in, but they will also keep Robbie. But I can't tell my parents that, can I?

So I tried a different line of attack.

"What happened to being nice to people?" I hit back, my tone letting them know that I, their only son, was totally disappointed in their failure to live up to my expectations. I swear sometimes I can be a real smartass too. Like father, like son.

My parents looked at each other. I know that look. It means, people, we have a situation here.

But I realized my dad could be as stubborn as he could be sarcastic.

'We are being nice to people," He insisted. "Nice to Robbie. He will be better off with people who know how to handle these matters."

"He has no family. He has nobody to care for him. You think the cops are going to do that?" Now I was playing for sympathy, having failed to move them with sarcasm. Appeal to the audience's sense of guilt and fairness, as Miss Faith says, when doing Language Analysis.

"They know how to handle it." My father was standing his ground.

"He won't go to them. He will run away, maybe slit his wrists or something. Then you will see!" The guilt card is falling heavily now.

"You are behaving like a silly boy!"

"So are you!" I cried. Now it was clear that the appeal to sympathy and guilt was failing, hitting a brick wall. That made me angry. And tearful.

"You are nothing but hypocrites! We must be nice to people! Be good to others and others will be good to us! What a load of crap!"

I could not believe I said it. I had never spoken to my parents like that. I did not realise it then but Robbie had changed me a lot. It took a crisis like this to bring it out.

"Shehan!" My mother's voice rose to a higher pitch. The highest, often reserved for emergencies like this.

"Go to your room!"

She didn't have to tell me. I was already on my way. And by the time I reached the top of the stairs the tears were well on their way.

I shut the door and fell on my bed. Why the fuck can't they understand? Robbie will not have a chance anywhere else. Here he will be at home. And he will be with me. A dream was going to come true and my parents had to ruin it. How can they be so cruel?

I must have been lying there for a long time. I didn't want to call Robbie. I had wanted to get my parents agree to my brilliant plan and then break the good news to Robbie. Now there was no news for him. No plan. No ideas.

Then I heard a knock on the door. I opened my eyes. It was dark. I must have been lying in bed for a long time.

The knock came again. It had to be Dad. What the hell was he knocking for? The door is not locked.

Then I heard the door open and his footsteps inside.

I pretended to be asleep. But it doesn't work with him.

"You can wake up now," he said, sitting on the bed. I opened my eyes but didn't turn around.

"You really want him here don't you?"

I said nothing.

"Is it as bad as you say?"

Still nothing from me.

"You must tell the truth, Shehan. Is Robbie's father really the monster you say he is?"

I shifted slightly in my position. "He is more than that", I said, sensing some softening in the opposition's stance. "He is the worst..."

"There! There! No swearing." A pre-emptive strike.

"I believe you," Dad said after a short pause. "We both believe you. If you are lying then it's your problem."

Once again, put the ball in my court. Nice work Dad.

"Is there something else you want to tell me?"

"Something else?"

"I mean about Robbie."

What is he talking about? Does he want me to tell him that I have a crush on him? Surely he can't expect me to be that honest? Besides, didn't he already know that?

"They showed that guy who was bashed again a little while ago. And the picture of the guy who bashed him. I can't help but think that he looks a lot like Robbie after all."

I froze. It seemed that I was the only person who thought the little girl's picture was way off the mark.

I turned around. Dad was looking down at me, eyes gentle, but daring me to contradict him.

"I had nothing to do with it."

A thin smile spread on his lips.

"So Robbie did."

I cursed myself. My sense of self-preservation has betrayed Robbie.

I nodded, slightly. Inside I was feeling like shit.

"You have no idea what he is going through. When Gary bashes him he goes through these rages. Truly spastic."

"I am sure," Dad said. "I am sure. But that poor man is in hospital. Out of danger now, but still in hospital, probably traumatized for life. Not to mention what that poor girl and the rest of his family must be going through."

I lay back in bed. I couldn't think of anything to say.

"Does he want to give himself up? You know they will take his background into consideration."

"NOOOOO!" I sat up again. "No way! That will kill him. They will put him away and he will kill himself."

"They have people who can help him."

"They can't help him. I know him."

Dad looked away at the dark corner of the room. I felt I was gaining the advantage again.

"He just needs to stay away from trouble without being sent away."

Dad sighed, deeply, loudly. I could almost feel the air shaking.

"Alright," he said after a little while. "I can offer him a job at the garage, after school. You know how I sometimes work late after Chris goes home? Robbie can help me. He can learn the job. I am sure he is good with his hands."

He chuckled at his little joke. I told you he can be pretty weird sometimes.

But I felt relieved enough to smile.

"And he can live in the room at the back of the garage. Not permanently but until things settle down."

"Why not here?"

Dad looked at me with the strictest frown he could manage.

"Don't push it Shehan!" He said getting up. "That's the best deal I can offer."

I sighed again. Yes it was better than nothing. Robbie can be out of trouble and I can make regular trips to the garage. Yes it was a good deal, considering.

"Thanks Dad," I said after a pause. "You are the best."

A cheeky grin came to his lips. 'Oh I know," he said. 'I just want to be better".

He chuckled as he got up. If he was closer I would have hugged him.

"And that boy really needs some help." He said, looking at me. "Before he gets killed or before he kills somebody or both."

A chill crawled up my spine. It was a scary possibility. But my mind did not dwell too much on it. It turned swiftly to the matter at hand.

"But right now what he needs is to get away from Gary."

Dad nodded as he walked to the door. Near the door he stopped as if remembering something.

"Just one more thing," he said, half turning. "You still don't have a girlfriend, do you?"

* * *

When I broke the news to Robbie he was quite pleased.

"Good idea!" he said. "Thanks!"

And I was pleased too. The next best thing to Robbie living in our house was Robbie living in my father's garage.

<h1 style="text-align:center">Five</h1>

Robbie moved in a couple of days later in the evening, after school. But not before my parents had a family discussion with me.

Family discussions are pretty challenging things for kids in most homes because they usually mean that the kids are in trouble or are about to get into trouble. In our home, it is challenging for another reason. It is a moment when I am compelled to listen to my parents' philosophy, about the only time I am forced to do anything in our home. Usually, I get it in small doses, delivered rather casually, almost in passing. Dad could be saying there is enough greed in the world without us adding to it while washing his plate and Mum could be joining in as she wiped it, chirping that there is so much wealth in the world it is an outrage that there are so many poor people in it at all. All this because I asked why we couldn't have charged at least a hundred bucks for the old Datsun Dad gave free to Uncle Herath. Of course, they are not telling me that this is what I should believe. This is what they believe and I am free to follow – or not. And because the philosophy is given in the form of passing remarks you really feel you have a choice, of listening to or ignoring the remarks even though I am more likely to listen because there is no obligation, and I would feel shitty if I didn't because there was never any compulsion. I think this is their strategy too, to compel with a choice. But the feeling of genuine choice is always there. But a family discussion is different. It is one where you have to sit down in the lounge, with Dad on one side and Mum on the other, with no choice whatsoever and face the full blast of the philosophy - in large doses.

The last time I had to do it was like 10 years ago when I broke a very expensive dish which Mum had borrowed from a friend. I picked it up really casually and because I didn't bother to hold it properly it fell and broke into a million pieces. But the discussion was not because of the broken dish, not even because the watery prawn curry had splashed all over Mum's dress. The discussion was because I asked Mum why she was so upset when it was not even her dish? Boy! That nearly drove them over the edge! First they stared at me as if I had uttered the most profane thing imaginable. Then they sat me down in the lounge room and gave me this long lecture about how one should respect other people's property. Only really, really, REALLY selfish people would destroy other people's stuff and not even worry about it. But, naturally, having heard all this, I was free to do as I wished but just imagine, Dad asked finishing the discussion on a high philosophical note, if that was your phone that was dashed on the floor!

So that night, the night I had the argument with Dad and Dad agreed to let Robbie live in the garage, we had another family discussion. Usual form, me sitting between them, Mum was sitting real close so that she could stroke my head. Normally I love it when she does that because she normally does it when I have a headache and it is so damn soothing when her fingers run through my hair. But that night it was giving me a headache because I knew what the discussion was gonna be about. And it wasn't the kind of headache that would go away because Mum stroked my head.

Dad did not beat about the bush. "You do understand," he began, "That what Robbie did was very serious?"

I nodded. That was no trick question. Of course, I knew it was serious. We all knew it. I am sure even Robbie knew it. It was just that we couldn't do anything about it.

"You are lucky that man is out of danger. If something bad had happened to him you would all be in trouble," Mum chipped in. "As it is you *should* have been in trouble considering what Robbie did to him."

I said nothing. If the aim was to make me feel uncomfortable and even scared it was working like magic.

"Robbie staying here is only going to help in the short run, you know that don't you?" Dad asked again. "He needs help. Badly. He needs to see someone."

"He already has," I said, glad to have something of my own to say at last. "He spoke to the school counsellor. Didn't work."

"Maybe he needs to find something or someone that works," Mum said. Again, I retreated into silence.

For a while, they both said nothing, as if waiting for me to say something. When it was clear that I was not going to, Dad started again. "And you young man," he said, his tone assuming a sudden firmness. "You need to think very seriously of your role in all this."

I looked at him in surprise. Was he suggesting that I also bashed the Afghan?

"My role?"

Dad nodded.

"Well, you are his friend, you hang out with him, what Robbie does is your responsibility as well."

Mum kissed my head. It would have been really sweet if the circumstances were different.

"If you are a good friend you ought to be able to influence him. If you don't, I am afraid you will end up being like him very soon."

I opened my mouth to say that trying to influence Robbie hasn't worked either but realized that it would only prolong the discussion. So I nodded again.

"Good," said Dad, getting up to signal the end of the discussion. He delivered his philosophical advice as he got up. "It is entirely up to you what you do with your life but remember you might want to seriously consider whether Robbie should be like you or whether you should end up like him."

That was a very cryptic way to end the discussion. Was he suggesting that I too could end up bashing people? Me? Bashing? It was too ridiculous to even think about. So I forgot about it quickly. Besides I had more important things to occupy my mind. Robbie was coming to stay in the garage.

* * *

Robbie came to the garage at about 5.30 in the evening. He brought just a bag of clothes. The room was at the back of Dad's garage, a little self-contained joint with a bed, a bar fridge, some basic furniture and a little shower cubicle and toilet. There was even a little microwave and a tiny electric stove with a single burner and some pots and pans and cutlery if one wanted to do some cooking. After Angelo left a couple of years ago no one had lived there and Dad had turned it into a kind of storeroom. The day before Robbie moved in Dad cleaned it up and prepared it for Robbie: clean sheets on the bed, all the paper and shit removed from the cupboard and an old colour TV installed on the little table. The bathroom and toilet were cleaned and fresh towels were put in. The bar fridge was still working and he put in a few complimentary coke cans in it. I helped him with the enthusiasm of a kid engaged in his favourite hobby.

"Think that'll do?" Dad asked me after we had finished. I nodded.

It was basic, yes, but it would be enough for Robbie under the circumstances.

"I guess the shower is not really necessary."

Dad could not resist it I guess.

"Dad! Please!"

"Alright, alright. Just kidding." He laughed. "I hope he will be happy here."

So did I. As for me, I was already over the moon.

Dad went home at about 5 in the evening asking me to stay and show Robbie to his new home. Robbie came about half an hour later, dressed in jeans, a dirty windcheater and sneakers, carrying just an old backpack full of clothes. He saw me and flashed a tired but happy smile.

"There you are!" I cried. "Welcome to your new home!"

Robbie was quite impressed with the set-up. "Looks fucking great!" He said, throwing his bag on the bed. He immediately started texting Sarah.

I noticed the ugly bruise on the side of his face. Dark and ugly, smirching that handsome face more than any dirt could. There was even a little bit of hardened blood on it. Gary must be the worst asshole in the world.

While Robbie punched his message on the phone I went into the bathroom, filled the bowl with some warm water and brought it with a face towel. I dipped the towel in the water and squeezed the excess water out.

Robbie stopped texting and looked at me questioningly.

"That bruise looks bad," I said. "Let me dab it with this water. It will make a difference."

Robbie looked confused at this sudden offer but did not say anything. He did not protest when I knelt before him and started dabbing the bruise with the warm, wet towel.

I began to wash the blood and dirt away, gently, carefully. And as I did Robbie winced from the pain and a tear escaped his eyes and trickled over the bruise. Then another, and another. I continued to clean, wiping away blood, dirt and tears, fighting my own tears ready to stream out. I washed and I cleaned, like a mother tending to a child, a nurse to a patient, a wife to her husband.

Suddenly Robbie grabbed my arm tightly. The bruise was stinging too much.

"Oww!' He cried. "Watch it! You're fucking hurting me!'

He was annoyed but I couldn't help smiling. God, he looked so handsome, with his face cleaned up, the full lips slightly open to reveal those white teeth.

"Finally," I said, "I can see your face properly."

His eyes lit up with anger and he gripped my arm tightly. I was regretting the stupid quip when he saw it for what it was. The grip slackened, the eyes closed and the lips spread into a warm smile. Just like on that day when I turned the hose on him. The kind of smile you have when you realise that you have been pissed off at something you should have been laughing at. A smile of quiet realization, of acceptance. But above all a smile that shows that despite all the pain that is crawling inside, you can still see the funny side of things. The sweetest smile of all.

I continued to wash and clean. There were no further interruptions.

* * *

I lived the next few days as if in a dream. Robbie was with me. Well, not exactly with me but I figured him living in the garage down the road from our house was as good as him living with me.

After school I walked back with Robbie and while he went to the garage I went home. I had a quick snack and flew to the garage. Robbie would be there already at work helping Dad. By the time I got to the garage, Robbie would be under a car or bending over an open bonnet. And I would wait till he finished, watching him while he worked, gazing at the blond hair bouncing around, the long arms straining. He was usually quiet when Dad was around but if we were alone he would ask me to give him a hand with some small job, which I was only too glad to do. "Why dontcha learn a job like this?" He would tease me sometimes. "Plenty of money in it. More than you can make by going to Uni and shit." I would smile and say that I was not as good with my hands as he was.

The first couple of days Dad got me to give them a hand as well. Not big jobs, just cleaning up and maybe tightening a few bolts. But it came to an end when I broke a bolt, trying to tighten it too much, much to Robbie's amusement. "You definitely have a few screws to tighten up here," he said, chuckling, playfully smacking my head. Dad wasn't amused though. He sent me promptly back to just cleaning up.

Sometimes I would go to the little room at the back and tidy it up. Put the clothes on the wall hanger and make the bed which Robbie always left in a mess. I would also take the empty coke cans and drop them in the bin outside. Sometimes I would even sweep the floor and mop the little bathroom. I was loving my role, keeping Robbie's room neat and tidy. But it irritated Robbie to see me doing that. What the fuck are you doing that for? He would ask and I would simply say it was good to have a tidy room and that if he didn't do it somebody had to do it. I did not say that I liked doing it for him. Well, he said, tidy your own fucking room, but did nothing to stop me either. So I continued to do what I liked doing.

I guess in my mind I was playing housewife, to Robbie, in our little home. I even toyed with the idea of cooking something for him. Nothing too flash – you can't do much on a single burner – but something simple but memorable, like a nice juicy steak. Buy one with my pocket money on the way from home to the garage, and cook it after Dad had gone. But it was too much to dare. Somehow I felt that Robbie would feel hugely embarrassed if I did that. I did not have the guts to find out how much.

Dad was pleased with Robbie. He was a good worker, he said at dinner one night. And he can speak. I smiled tiredly at this lame remark and asked him what he spoke about. Dad said nothing much, only what he had to in order to do the work but that was sufficient to know that he could speak. And as usual, he laughed at his own lame joke and ruffled my hair to show that he did not mean any harm.

Mum was wondering if we should ask him to come to dinner one night, to sample some of her curries or even mine. But Dad thought it was too early. Let the boy be domesticated in the garage first, he said, laughing again at his own weird sense of humour. But I was also glad that they didn't invite him. It would have only embarrassed poor Robbie. After Robbie moved into the garage I realized what a big mistake it would have been if he had come to live with us, in the house. He would have been totally out of place, not knowing what to do with the environment he found himself in. That would have been as cruel as letting him live with Gary.

Dad, however, took the idea of 'domesticating' Robbie seriously. At work, he would ask Robbie to wash his hands and face regularly without making it appear too obvious and once even asked him to use soap. But Dad was not satisfied with cleansing Robbie's hands; he was also keen to cleanse Robbie's mind and soul. I have heard Dad say that the Buddha had tamed many angry and nasty people with a few wise and gentle words. I guess Dad probably thought if Buddha could do it so could he but I wasn't sure if the Buddha had dealt with anyone like Robbie. But Dad was not to be put off. One evening Robbie was taking a break with a coke and I saw Dad going up to him and sitting next to him on one of the milk crates we used for seats. I realized something very interesting was about to happen but didn't know what until Dad opened his mouth.

"So Robbie," he started. "Shehan tells me that you got a bit of a temper."

Robbie looked at me sitting on the floor just a few feet from him as if he wanted to do a demonstration right then and there.

I guess I should have told Dad what happened to Mr. Wilmot's counselling efforts. But I didn't. I was too interested in seeing how Dad handled this.

Dad soldiered on. "We all have our moments I guess," he continued. "Moments when we think we can't hold it in anymore. When we need to pour it out and free ourselves. But how we choose to do is entirely up to us. We may choose to release our anger in ways that hurt others and ourselves or we may choose to do it in other less harmful, more creative ways."

He looked at me and saw my amusement. It did not deter him though. I gotta hand it to Dad. He is persistent.

"At the end of the day, it is your life, you have to live it. We can't tell you how to live it but we can tell you what we think may happen if you choose to live it the wrong way."

All this time Robbie was not saying anything. He was just sipping his coke and glancing at me, clearly pissed off with me for telling my father about his anger issues, and at the same time looking for a release for his anger I guess. My obvious amusement only seemed to increase it. Finally, tired of Dad's sermon, he got up and picked up the spanner he had been using. For a moment I thought he was about to use it for something other than tightening a bolt.

"Alright," he said to Dad. "Which screws you want me to tighten next?"

Dad stared at Robbie probably wondering which screws he meant, the real screws in the car they were fixing or some figurative screws in Dad's head. But he recovered quickly to point out the screws in the car. For the next few minutes Robbie went into a frenzy of screw tightening, I am sure all the time imagining that they were in Dad's head.

That night over dinner I told Mum what happened. She was in stitches. "Serves you right for trying your philosophy on everyone", she said. "It works with some, with others it doesn't."

But Dad was adamant that it worked because Robbie chose to express his anger by doing something productive, like tightening the screws in the car.

* * *

Robbie finished work around six and after work, we headed back to the station. I was hoping we could meet in the garage. But Robbie preferred the railway station. That was where he was used to being. I swear he would have preferred to live there. He seemed to be drawn to those tracks.

Besides, Dad too insisted that we did not meet in the garage. I remember that first evening Sarah came bouncing into the garage thrilled that Robbie had his own little pad. But Dad would have none of that. It was a place of work, he said firmly. Not a social club. I guess he was worried about opening his business premises to the whims of a bunch of teenagers, even though he trusted his son one hundred per cent.

You could always come home and chat, Dad said once but Robbie just scrunched up his face and said "Nah, we're alright." By now Dad has learned to read Robbie's body language well. He simply shrugged his shoulders and said just lock the doors before you go.

So we continued to meet at the station, doing the usual – nothing. The first couple of days Sarah fussed over Robbie's bruise saying he should show it to a doctor and Robbie asked her to just shut the fuck up because it wasn't hurting anymore.

There was also a downside to Robbie moving in. My Dad was now able to observe me and Robbie more closely and if any proof of my devotion to Robbie was needed he got plenty during that week. More than once I saw him looking at me sweeping the room and making Robbie's bed with eyes that were even more troubled than Robbie's when he told me not to do it.

Maybe that is why he wanted to have another serious chat with me one night, after dinner. A serious chat about my future.

He called me to the lounge where he sat with Mum, the TV turned off. He asked me to sit on the sofa and looked at Mum as if checking with her if it was ok to commence. Having received the desired level of consent he commenced.

"Have you thought about what you want to do with your life?"

Shit, I thought. Here it comes. My Buddhist, liberal parents are finally becoming Sri Lankan. Wanting me to be an astronaut or a pharmacist.

"I don't want to be a pharmacist," I said weakly.

Dad smiled and looked at Mum who also smiled. Guess they thought it was all very cute.

"We don't want you to be anything you don't want to be," Dad said. 'We just want to know whether you have given it any thought."

I thought a bit. That was the first time I had been required to think about it in a long time. I had never really given much thought to my future, not lately anyway. When we got together at the station we rarely talked about these things; the conversation was on the present rather than the future. That is all that seemed to matter. And I had rarely thought about it on my own. With Robbie around, my present was fine and I kind of thought that the future would take care of itself. If anything, the future made me worried. I must admit that when I was in Year Eleven I had a vague idea that I wanted to go to TAFE and do a hospitality course so that I could follow my love of cooking. I even pictured myself being a chef in some big hotel cooking all kinds of new and exotic dishes, maybe even having my own TV show. Then with Robbie coming into my life all that had changed. Cooking was now on the back burner. TAFE also became more like a threat than a prospect. It would mean not being able to see

Robbie too often. If going to Uni or TAFE now came into the picture it was only as an extension of the present. I would go to Uni or TAFE but only if I could go there with Robbie. Sounds a bit far-fetched I know but I wanted to believe that it was possible.

But Uni was the last thing Robbie was interested in. I remember trying a few times to get him interested in the idea, always with the same result.

"Why the fuck would I wanna go to Uni for?" He would ask. "If you wanna go, you go!"

He seemed immovable, like a rock. He had set his eyes on getting a job as soon as possible, like an apprenticeship. Then getting his own pad and moving his mum and Megan there. Uni was not going to help him with that.

So, I began to think, since Robbie doesn't want to go to Uni and I want to be with him, maybe I shouldn't go to Uni too.

And that is what I told Dad.

"I am not sure if I wanna go to Uni," I said apologetically. It felt kinda painful to say that. I knew despite all their philosophy my parents wanted to see me study beyond school, even if it was TAFE. If you want to be a chef that is fine, good money in it and an honest, creative job, Dad had said. But remember education doesn't end with school.

"Uni is boring." I continued my Uni bashing. "Four or five more years of study. I'd rather get some job or even an apprenticeship."

Mum and Dad shared that 'we have a situation' look. "Like Robbie you mean?" Dad asked. Smartass!

"Yeah." I shrugged. "Maybe."

Dad's voice was becoming very serious now. "Listen," he started. "We don't want to tell you how to live your life. It's your life. But we have a duty to tell you what we think is good for you. If you want to do what Robbie does, fine. But does Robbie know what he wants to do?"

That was a good question. Robbie didn't. He just went from job to job, fight to fight.

I shrugged my shoulders again.

"He will do something today and something else tomorrow. He doesn't care. He is used to it. But before you know it you will find that you are chasing something you can never get and that you are stuck in a rut, frustrated and bored."

That is the closest they ever came to discussing my crush on Robbie. And when they put it like that, chasing something you can't get, it hurt. Like a big rock dropping on my heart from a great height.

"And not to mention that boy's violent habits," Mum joined in now. "Next time he bashes somebody he may do some real harm and you may end up in prison with him."

"Or in the hospital," Dad said. "Robbie may not get away with things all the time"

"If that is what you want, then fine. But think carefully of the consequences. You will always be our son no matter what. But it would hurt us a lot if you get hurt."

That was the end of the little chat. But it had the intended effect like all little philosophical chats did. It made me feel bad.

I spent that night thinking of what Dad said. I don't know why but it had touched me like no other little chat had done. Was it because it touched some concern I've always had deep down about what I was involved in? Was I getting too hung up on Robbie for my own good? Was I, as Dad said, chasing something I couldn't get? What if next time Robbie bashed someone and landed in jail? It had come quite close to that this time with the Afghan. If something bad had happened to him things would have become very serious. I guess I was too blinded by Robbie's blond hair and handsome face to see it. But I admit it did appear scary for a moment. Me getting stuck in some boring job, even more boring than Uni with Robbie gone somewhere and my future gone forever, not to mention Robbie who had moved on. Or what if Robbie does something really rash and we both end up in jail?

No, I tried to tell myself. It can never be that bad. Never. And all I needed to convince myself that it was just a baseless fear, invented by my parents to keep me away from Robbie was to picture Robbie's face and that dazzling smile.

* * *

My dad was right though. Robbie's stay at the garage did not last long. A week to be exact. And it ended in a painful way.

He was not feeling very comfortable, I could see that. I had come to know him very well now; I knew when he was worried, when he was happy, when he was thinking and when he was just staring at something without thinking. I probably knew that more than Sarah did. And those days he was doing a lot of staring without thinking.

"What's the matter?" I asked him one day, seeing him gazing vacantly at the street outside. It was late morning on Sunday. I had gone to the garage to see him straight after breakfast to find him in this mood.

He said nothing. But I could see that he was troubled. I stopped making the bed and looked at him.

"I wanna go home."

He said simply. I could say from his tone that he was unhappy. The voice sounded flat, without life. The face betrayed the pain inside.

"I wanna see Mum and Megan."

He must have been thinking about it ever since he came here, I thought. Wondering what they were doing, how little Megan was getting on, whether she had been to school, or done her home work because his mum was too preoccupied with her own sorrows and Gary with delivering those sorrows to worry about Megan.

I did not know what to say. I could appreciate his worry. But Robbie going home was not the smartest thing right now. Home was where he got bashed. Besides, and perhaps more than anything else, I guess I did not want to see him leave the garage. It was way too soon for the dream to end.

"I am sure they'll be alright," I said, trying hard to sound convincing. "Better to stay here for a while and go when things settle down."

"How the fuck do you know if they'll be alright?" He asked, indignantly. "You don't live there!"

He suddenly got up and started stuffing his clothes into his bag.

"I am leaving," he said, zipping the bag up. He had made up his mind. Just like that.

I stood there dumbfounded, unable to believe that he was really leaving. So suddenly. So soon. He looked at me and saw the worry in my eyes.

"Don't be such a pussy!" He said. He appeared tired of my attitude. "I will see ya tonight at the station."

But that did nothing for me. Now all the joy I had of having Robbie there was to end, so suddenly, after just one week. It was too much too soon. I guess I was behaving like a jilted lover. But at the time I did not realise it. Maybe I didn't care either. All I felt was the hurt and the hopelessness.

"How could you?!" I heard myself asking, half crying, voice breaking. "After everything I did for you!"

I guess I couldn't help that. My heart was doing all the thinking and talking now.

But the accusation made Robbie start. He looked at me in disbelief for a few moments as if trying to figure out if I was serious. One look at my face would have convinced him that I was beyond serious. I was Desperate. Then those thick, full lips curled into a strange smile. A smile of contempt.

"Oh yeah?" He asked, staring straight at me. "You did all this for me huh? Not because you enjoyed washing my face? Making my bed? Tidying my room? What was it gonna be next? Jumping in bed with me?"

The words hit me like a brick and left me reeling. My legs wobbled, my feet felt cold. I felt like I was in some big park, naked in broad daylight with people staring at me, laughing their heads off. I wanted to disappear. But I couldn't.

So I sheepishly raised the eyes I had lowered to look at him.

Robbie was angry but he was also shaking. Was he shaking because he was angry or because he had seen what his words had done to me? I was not sure. I guess I wanted to believe the latter. I wanted to look at his eyes, to see if he had seen mine, the tears welling in them, to see if he was hurt to see the pain he had caused. But he turned his eyes away, abruptly, and picked up the bag.

Then he walked out, still turning his eyes away from mine, his sneakers beating a sad rhythm out of the garage.

I spent the rest of the day sulking. I told Dad that Robbie had left. He simply shrugged his shoulders and said it was fine.

Maybe the boy missed his family. He will have to find somebody else to do the work. Or maybe he could do it on his own. I am sure he wasn't unhappy. I was glad that he did not say 'I told you so.' That was not his style.

But I wished I could be as calm as Dad about it. Robbie had left and he had called me a fag. Not exactly in those words but the meaning was clear. And when he said that his eyes were filled with an anger that made me shudder.

Clearly, he knew about my crush. For how long? Did he also hate it? Was that simply anger in his eyes or hate? I could not figure it out. But I swear it made me feel like shit. To be crushed by my crush, to have my affection thrown at my face like that. The more I thought about it, the more humiliated I felt.

No, I thought. I shouldn't demean myself like this. I shouldn't let Robbie treat me like this, no matter how hot he was.

So I made a decision. I will not have anything to do with Robbie anymore. If he hates me for being a fag then I don't want to have anything to do with him. I may be a fag but I have my dignity.

Never again. I said to myself. Never again will I hang out with Robbie McMillan.

Dad was right. I am chasing something I can't get. Someone who does not care about hurting me.

I guess I was behaving like a teenager with a broken heart, rejected and humiliated, vowing revenge out of hurt rather than hate.

I had lunch in front of the TV and went upstairs to my room. I had two essays to finish. I will do them now. Hereafter my studies will take priority.

I was halfway through the first essay when the mobile rang. It was Robbie.

"We are at the station." He was trying to sound annoyed, I could say. But his voice shook, slightly, as if he was uncertain of himself. "Why the fuck aren't ya here?"

I opened my mouth to tell him about my decision but I guess subconsciously I had been expecting the call all the time I was telling myself that I was not going back to Robbie. That was probably why I had not turned the mobile off despite my resolution.

So I told him I would see him in ten minutes. The essay could wait. Robbie McMillan deserved another chance.

* * *

Life returned to normal. We continued to meet by the tracks, catch the odd movie and talk loads of crap.

There was no further violence from Gary. At least for the time being. Robbie never said anything but he had no more bruises, at least not ones we could see. His mum and Megan were fine, he said. He had even taken Megan to see a movie, and then to Mcdonalds.

The little spat I had with Robbie was forgotten. Or never talked about. I guess it was embarrassing for both of us. I had convinced myself that Robbie didn't really mean what he said. We were still meeting as usual and a little bit of pain now and then, I told myself, was a small price to pay for being with him.

I never got to know how Robbie felt about it. But I could sense that something had changed in him towards me. For instance at school during lunch he would skip playing footy now and then and come and sit with me and chat, telling me about some funny thing Megan or Sarah did or how he was pissed off at somebody at work or something else like that. Then one day at a movie I beat Marty to the seat next to Robbie and Marty just muscled in and shoved me away. Robbie promptly ordered Marty to back off and sit somewhere else and the pushy little prick was not game enough to disobey. But the best and sweetest indication of Robbie's changed attitude was a silly discussion we had about Girls.

Marty started it, talking about some chick he had been fooling around with in a car park. We were by the tracks as usual; Robbie on the bench, in customary pose with back to the lamp post, hugging Sarah who sat huddled between his long legs. Marty at the other end of the bench, me and Mark on the ground. Empty coke bottles and fag ends all around us.

Marty was talking about the chick's legs, her breasts, her hair, not caring if Sarah was there and Sarah was laughing the loudest when Marty said that the girl was not wearing a bra.

"How old was she?"

Mark asked, eyes gleaming.

"Dunno." Marty said. "20 maybe."

"You're fucking kidding?" Mark was very impressed. You could see that in his eyes and feel it in his tone.

Then he dug me in the ribs with his elbow. "See what you are missing out on?"

Everybody laughed. Even Robbie was smiling though he was not looking at me. I felt my cheeks burning.

"Really, Shehan, why dontcha find a chick?" Sarah asked, looking down at me from her comfort between Robbie's legs. "I am sure there are lots of chicks that you like"

"Are there?" Marty asked and again everybody laughed. Robbie's smile broadened though he still did not look at me.

"You don't wanna be like fucking twenty and find that all the hot chicks are taken," Mark said, winking at Marty.

I just sat there saying nothing hoping the conversation would turn to something else, powerless to make it happen.

"By then you will have only boys to chase after," Again raucous laughter. But now Robbie was not smiling anymore.

"Maybe he is saving it for the right person."

Everybody looked at Robbie. There was a finality in his tone, a tone everybody recognised as the signal to change the conversation.

I looked up at Robbie. He was now looking straight at me, arms hugging Sarah closer, chin resting on her shoulder, a faint smile playing on his lips and his eyes filling with warmth.

Then the teeth flashed. I melted.

Six

The days rolled on, like the trains that came and went. I went through my usual routine. School, home, Robbie.

At school, however, things were getting intense. This was year Twelve. Exams were getting closer and the teachers were getting agitated. Actually, I think some of them were more worried than the kids. At least more worried than me.

I was not doing too badly but I could have also been doing way better. Only If I had paid my studies half the attention I have been paying to Robbie.

My parents were also getting slightly worried. But true to his philosophy Dad put no pressure on me, even if my less philosophical mum was putting subtle pressure on him to make me work harder. "We can only tell you what we think is right," he said, whenever I told them a SAC mark which they thought could have been improved. "But at the end of the day, it's your life. But don't say that we didn't warn you." He would glance at Mum and Mum would give him that 'I don't quite agree with you' look. Pressure, Mum style.

Then to make matters worse, Robbie got expelled.

He was in a punch-on for maybe the fiftieth time since he came to school and this time the teachers saw him. We were walking down the corridor during recess one day and this kid, a tall but skinny bloke called Gavin who had just started hitting the weights at the local gym said something to Robbie, something about a little boy getting bashed by his dad. I guess Gavin should have waited until he got a bit bigger before he said that because Robbie promptly turned around and showed him who the little boy really was. Soon Gavin was picking two of his teeth from the floor to take to the office to complain and while he was on his way to the office Mr. Jackson who was on yard duty ran to the scene and from a safe distance ordered Robbie to follow Gavin to the office. It was later said that Robbie was trapped, provoked into having a fight when teachers were around. If it was so Gavin paid a heavy price. But Robbie's punishment was heavier. He had to go.

He was not worried. He was thinking of dropping out anyway I guess and Gary I was told, didn't take it seriously either. He had been telling Robbie to get out of school and get a job. In fact, Robbie seemed to feel very pleased about the whole deal. He walked out of school giving high fives to everybody.

But I was devastated. I could not see him at school anymore. Even though he was often absent from school it was never like this. I admit, it was hard when he didn't turn up; but I always knew that he would turn up eventually, if not the next day then the following day. But now he was gone from the school forever. Will I also not be able to see him at the station? Will he go to another school now, find another group of friends and hang out somewhere else? I could not figure out what I would do if that happened.

Life became miserable now. For two days I didn't hear from

him; my text messages were not answered, and when I called, his phone was turned off. Neither Marty nor Mark heard from him and he was not to be found at the station. Even Sarah had not heard from him, according to Marty. I spent most of my time at school daydreaming and scribbling on paper, thinking of Robbie, wondering where he was and wishing he was there, sitting next to me, drawing funny faces of teachers in his book. I wished I could be where he was, wherever it may be. At home, it was no different. I told my parents I had homework and spent most of my time in the room, in bed, thinking, longing. The longing was so strong that I even thought of changing schools to wherever Robbie went, or even just dropping out and getting a job with Robbie. I swear I did if that was the only way I could be with Robbie.

But Robbie did not go to another school. I heard from him after a couple of days, after school. He was at the station, waiting for everybody.

I flew to the station. There he was, sitting on the bench, beaming. I went up to him and he offered his fist for me to punch.

"God, Robbie!" I said, breathless. "I thought you were gone!"

He said nothing but half-closed his eyes and smiled.

Two minutes later Sarah came on the train on the other track, crossed the tracks and rushed to Robbie. "Ya fucking bastard!" She cried with joy and he wrapped her in his long arms and kissed her. I stood there looking away at the railway tracks, trying to imagine what Robbie's lips were doing to Sarah's. She was the lucky one. But I was lucky too, I thought. Robbie was back.

Within a few minutes, the others turned up and we all went to get some Maccas. Robbie told us that he had completely dropped out of school and had started looking for work. But we would continue to meet at the station, he had decided, to my great joy.

It was only later that I realized that I had worried for nothing. He had nowhere else to go. The station had become like a second home to him. But at the time I was just happy that he was back.

Again, life returned to normal.

But not completely. The loss I felt when Robbie was gone had shaken me. It was that crushing fear of losing the one person dearest to you and not knowing what to do about it. The kind of loss that leaves you empty inside and numb all over. Panic attack of the emotional kind.

And from somewhere within, a small voice was beginning to call now. The voice of my parents. You will soon realise you are chasing after something you can never have. Then what?

Sometimes, during those couple of days when I was at school feeling lonely and lost after Robbie left, wishing he had been there, I did think about it, where all this was leading, feeling so depressed about not having Robbie around, how it felt as if it was like the end of everything for me. What was I expecting to do with my infatuation? Where was I expecting to go with it? Did I really think I was going to be with Robbie forever? Clearly, he was no fag and did not feel the same way about me, even if he definitely had a soft spot for me. It was Sarah he hugged and cuddled and kissed. He would settle down with a girl, if not Sarah then someone else. What was I going to do? Live in his basement?

These were questions too hard to answer and I soon gave up trying. When Robbie returned to the station the questions retreated to the background and I always returned to my consolation that Robbie, despite not being a fag, really liked me and cared for me. Surely that warm smile when I told him I had thought he was gone forever was a definite sign of his appreciation of my loyalty and devotion? Perhaps there was even a chance of something more than that, eventually? I guess I liked to believe that.

But my parents' voice seemed to have taken hold of a small corner of my heart, constantly saying in a small but increasingly audible voice: you will find that you are chasing after something you can never get. I hoped it would go away but it didn't.

Then, things took a scary turn, giving my life a terrible jolt.

We were at the station going through the usual motions of killing time. It was late, like 8.00 in the evening. Marty and Mark hadn't turned up and Sarah was having some family thing. It was just me and Robbie, sitting around, talking crap. Robbie had finished telling me what he thought of Marty and Mark who had not turned up that night and had then started a long monologue on what he wanted to do to Asian women. Apparently there was an Asian woman who was Sarah's supervisor at work who was supposed to be a bitch. Robbie was coming up with all kinds of horrible things he wanted to do to them. But good old Robbie was faithful to Sarah even in his murderous thoughts. He wanted to do so many terrible things to Asian women but rape was not one of them. I told him that there were so many Asian women in the world he would soon run out of bullets if we decided to shoot them. He said he would have killed enough by then to scare the others away. We both laughed. It was crap but you got to admit it, it was funny crap.

Trains were coming and going and we paid no attention to them. I sat with Robbie, listening to him, making the odd comment or remark, stealing glances at his handsome figure and feeling the electricity of his presence. Even in the dark he looked handsome. Magnificent. And each time he smiled his teeth flashed like magic.

A train came in and halted. People were getting out, not many, just a handful as it was getting late. We glanced lazily at the train and continued our conversation which had now turned to what to do with the Asian men once Robbie had finished with their women.

Then I saw something. Somebody was gesturing wildly, frantically, in our direction from inside the train. Curious, I looked carefully and saw a girl, a little girl no more than 6 or 7 pointing at us and speaking madly to people around her. Of course we could not hear what she was saying. It was like watching something on TV with the volume turned down. But it was pretty clear she was talking about us.

Then it hit me. It was her! The little girl 0n the train the day Robbie bashed the Afghan! The Afghan's little daughter who stopped Robbie in his tracks. There she was, on the train right in front of us, and recognising Robbie, pointing him out to others. I guess she could recognize the guy who attacked her dad anywhere, especially if he was sitting under the light like Robbie did, in full view of everybody. And the people around her, Arab-looking, and young, were staring at us, getting agitated all the time.

I looked at Robbie. He was paying no attention to the drama before him, busy texting Sarah. He probably didn't even realise that there was a train in front of us.

I nudged him. He looked up, irritated.

"What?"

I pointed at the train. It was leaving now, the girl was still pointing at us and some of the men around her were moving towards the door. Evidently, they wanted to get out.

None of this registered with Robbie of course. He was simply pissed off that I interrupted his texting.

"What the fuck is wrong with you?"

"It's the girl!" I said, breathless, pointing at the train which was pulling away now. I could see the Afghans crowding around the door, gesturing menacingly, obviously disappointed at not being able to get out.

"What girl?"

"The Arab girl! The girl in the train the day you bashed that bloke!"

Then it clicked inside his head. The girl in the train! The girl in the train! Suddenly he looked as if woken from a dream.

"Where?"

"There! In the fucking train! She was showing us to some people. Other Arabs!" My voice was sounding frantic now.

Robbie's face clouded with worry. But he wasn't sure whether to believe it or not.

"Bullshit!" He said after a few moments of contemplation, obviously deciding not to believe it.

"You prolly saw someone else."

"I am telling ya!" I was beside myself now. "It was her! The girl. She was showing us to others! Other Arabs!" My god Robbie why can't you believe me?

"Calm down!" Robbie ordered. "You probably saw someone like her. You think you can recognise her? From here?"

"I will recognise her anywhere!" I cried" It was her! I swear!"

Robbie shook his head dismissively, he was getting tired of this now. He turned back to his texting. "So what?" He asked while punching letters. "The train's gone now."

I looked at him, sitting there texting his girlfriend as if nothing else mattered. The girl, the only person in the world who could recognise the attacker of her father had seen him and he was texting Sarah.

"What if they tell the cops?"

He looked up at me. "So what? They don't know who we are or where we live. They can't do shit."

"They will find out. I am sure of that." A chill was spreading down my spine. "Please Robbie," I pleaded. "Let's get outta here."

"You're getting paranoid," he said, still punching the message. "Relax! We'll go after I send this message."

I sighed looking away at the dark. Robbie seemed to be determined not to take this seriously. But I knew it was serious. I sensed it.

And I was right.

The Afghans did not go to the police. Instead, they came themselves.

We were about to leave the station. Robbie had just sent his message and we were walking towards the gate, the two of us in contrasting moods. Robbie pretty relaxed and me nearing panic stations.

Then the Afghans came.

Before we saw them, we heard them, chattering wildly and loudly in their language, the voices getting closer and closer down the ramp that led to the platform. The vices sounded excited and agitated, as if several people were trying to talk over each other.

Then we saw them. The moment I saw the shadows cantering down the ramp chattering in that language I realized who they were. The Afghans in the train! They must have got off the train at the next station and run all the way here to get us. I swear I could even hear some of them panting.

"What's wrong?" Robbie asked, seeing me stopping in my tracks. I tugged nervously at his arm.

"It's them!" I said in a whisper that shook with my nerves. "The Afghans! Run!"

Then it finally dawned on Robbie. Too late to avoid being seen by the mob but still with enough time to run. And he pulled me by my sleeve and turned and we both ran.

Behind us, the foreign language erupted into a frenzy of screams and the thud of feet picked up their menacing beat. The hunters had spotted their quarry and the chase was on.

We ran. Down the platform, as fast as we could. Naturally, Robbie was miles ahead of me, his long legs carrying him with ease. But he was always looking around, to see if I was following. And I was, as fast as my legs could carry me.

All kinds of horrible thoughts were running through my head. What if they catch us? What will they do to us? Will they kill us? Or just bash us? If they bash us how bad would it be? Shit!!! How the fuck did I get into this shit?!!

The footsteps were getting closer, my breath, shorter.

But something else was approaching us now, from the opposite direction. A train! I could see its lights creeping up the hedges on the side of the track and hear its engine above the Afghan screams. Then, it came into view, just around the corner inside the tunnel, two big yellow eyes getting bigger all the time.

I looked ahead at Robbie. He was at the corner of the platform, stopped, looking back at me and then at the train.

"Hurry!"

I looked back over my shoulder. The Afghans were just a mass of shadows growing ever closer. I could hear them, their voices and their feet thudding menacingly on the platform.

In front of us, the lights were getting bigger and brighter.

Robbie was still standing, looking at me. I suddenly realized what he was going to do. He was going to cross the track just before the train passed so that the train would cut in between us and the Afghans. Smart boy, My Robbie! But we had to be quick. The train was almost there.

I saw Robbie jump.

The long legs carried him across the tracks in two giant steps, and he scrambled up the platform on the other side.

"Hurry!" He yelled, standing up and gesturing madly.

I was opposite him now, standing. I wanted to jump but my feet wouldn't move. They stood as if nailed to the platform, the legs shaking as if wanting to spring out of my feet.

To my right, the Afghans closed in. I could even hear their breath now. To my left the train was blaring its horn, the lights blindingly bright. And before me, Robbie, now on his hands and knees on the platform, eyes pleading in the light of the train.

"Come on!" He cried. "Jump!"

I jumped.

The first thing I felt was the pain, an incredible piercing pain in my ankle. Then the leg gave way and I felt myself sinking, as if dropping into some bottomless hole. I felt myself falling on my side, on the gravel, in the middle of the tracks. I vaguely felt hitting my elbow on the track but by then the pain in the ankle was already climbing up the leg.

I lay there, holding my ankle, my vision blurred by pain and fear.

In front of me, the train was emerging from the tunnel.

I looked up and saw Robbie, at the edge of the platform, eyes wide with fear, screaming something.

I was not hearing a thing. Then everything went blank and merged with the darkness.

* * *

When I woke up I was in bed, in hospital. There was no Robbie, no Afghans. Only Mum and Dad standing over me.

"Ah, there you are! Back among the living."

Dad said, trying to smile. I say 'trying' because the lips moved awkwardly as if they were commanded to do something they couldn't.

I tried to smile too, with the same result.

"You had a narrow escape it seems," Mum said. She stroked my head and I could see the eyes moisten and the lips flutter.

"Fortunately, nothing broken."

Wow! I thought, remembering the pain. What a relief. I thought I had at least broken my ankle.

"Just a badly sprained ankle and severe pain. That is all." Dad said as if reading my thoughts.

"And bruises," Mum added.

"You must have passed out from the pain."

Yes, I thought. I remember the pain, and losing vision. And just before that, Robbie staring at me, in total fear.

But how did I get here? Where was Robbie?

"Where is Robbie?"

Mum and Dad looked at each other. Then they looked back at me in silence.

"Where is Robbie?"

My voice would have been raised as Mum and Dad looked slightly worried.

"He is fine," Mum said, squeezing my hand. "He is fine. Don't get tired."

"But where is he?"

My parents shared another glance. Then Dad told me the story. At least what Robbie had told him.

According to Robbie I had slipped and fallen on the way

home from the station, while crossing the road near the station, spraining my ankle as I was darting across the road to avoid an oncoming car. I had passed out from pain by the side of the road. Robbie had pulled me onto the footpath. Then he had brought me home.

"How did he bring me here?"

My father smiled, this time a real smile.

"He carried you," he said simply. "All the way from the station."

I could not help smiling. Robbie saved my life. Carried all the way from the station. I felt my eyes moisten and my chest tighten.

Dad's face now assumed a more serious expression.

"That's what he told us," he said. 'And we have no reason to doubt it. He carried you home. We were there when he brought you." Then he paused and exchanged another glance with Mum.

"But I am sure there is more to it than that." His voice and his look were stern now, as if daring me to contradict him.

I turned my gaze away from them. Obviously Robbie had not told them about the Afghans. Or the train. But did he tell them that he actually saved my life?

"You don't need to say anything now. Get some rest. We can talk later."

They left the room, my mother patting my head again and planting a kiss on my forehead before leaving.

I lay there thinking. I could not believe how close it had been. I could vaguely remember the train screaming down at me, the wheels dragging against the rails as the brakes were applied. In those few seconds before the train reached the spot I lay in, Robbie must have whisked me away. Into safety from a horrible death.

And then he carried me home. All the way from the station.

How did he get away from the Afghans? The last I remember of them was that they were running towards me, screaming and swearing, their footsteps menacingly close in the dark. I remembered nothing of them after I jumped. Heard nothing.

Maybe, I figured, they stayed on the platform, as the train cut them off from me and Robbie on the other side of the tracks, as Robbie had planned. But still, the train would have been there for only a few seconds. How did Robbie manage to get me – and himself – to safety?

I felt tired thinking about it. The important thing was that I was alive and Robbie too was fine. That was good enough for now. I could think about the rest later.

* * *

I was back home that evening. Robbie came to see me at home, around six. He came limping slightly but also smiling and gripped the hand I offered warmly. I noticed how his knuckles and fingers were bruised and cut.

"Thanks, mate," I said. "Thanks for saving my life."

Robbie just flashed his brilliant teeth. "For a little shit you are fucking heavy," was all he said. We both laughed.

"How ya feeling?"

"Good," I said. "Just the pain. Nothing broken."

"Good!" He said. "A few seconds delay and nothing would have been left."

He told me what happened. He had pulled me out onto the platform just in time and as he had expected, the train had cut us off from the Afghans. The train driver had thought that he had run me over and had stopped the train to investigate, giving Robbie more time to take me to safety. When he realized that I had passed out he carried me on his shoulder down the footpath that led along the tracks on the high ground and after walking for about two hundred meters re-crossed the tracks onto the other side, climbed the high ground through the scrub and then on to the road. Then he had carried me all the way home.

"Did you see the Afghans after that?" I asked, breathless.

"Not a fucking sight," Robbie said. "I think they chickened out after the train stopped."

I looked at him, a warmth filling my chest and my eyes. Robbie had pulled up his jumper sleeves and I saw his arms, scratched and cut horribly, ugly scars under that fine golden hair. He saw me looking and quickly pulled down the sleeves.

"How long ya gotta stay in bed?"

"Dunno. I guess at least a week. I can walk but with a limp."

Robbie grinned and nodded. He shifted on his feet and winced as he did. I suddenly remembered he too had walked in with a limp.

"What's with the leg Robbie," I asked, trying to raise myself on my elbow to see better.

"Nothing." He said, looking away. "Just a limp."

"How?"

He looked at me, irritated. "I don't fuckin' know. Just a limp. Don't fuckin' fuss about it."

I lay back in bed. What other pains and scars had he got to show for saving my life I wondered. The warmth in my eyes was fast melting into tears. I looked away at the window to hide it from him.

"Did Marty and Mark call?"

"Yeah. They said they couldn't make it today to see me but probably tomorrow."

Robbie sneered. "What do you expect!" He spat. "Selfish pricks. Probably have something more important!"

I said nothing. I never expected more than that from Marty and Mark anyway.

"How is Sarah?"

"She is ok," Robbie said, wincing again. "She's been buggin' me not to go to the station again. Afraid of the fucking Afghans."

I did not think it was a bad idea. The Afghans could be still prowling around.

"Maybe she is right," I said. "Maybe you should stay away from there at least for a while."

Robbie looked slightly annoyed. "I don't think they'll be coming there for long," he said. "They will probably give up after a week or so." God! He loved that station!

"But still," I tried to be insistent now. "Better to avoid it."

"Will you fucking give it a rest!" He was getting impatient, shifting on his feet and wincing.

"Just stop worrying and give it a rest."

Mum came in with a big glass of juice and a thick piece of chocolate cake. Robbie took the glass and mumbled a thanks. I saw Mum staring at the side of Robbie's face, the side that was shielded from my view, with wide eyes.

"That's a nasty scar you have got there Robbie," She said, glancing at me and raising her eyebrows in that 'what can you do?' expression. Robbie just kept gulping down the drink. I could see he was anxious.

"Have you shown it to somebody?"

He just nodded. "Nah," he said. "It's fine".

He turned to me. "I gotta go," he said, punching my fist in farewell. "Get better soon!"

Then he turned around and left.

Mum looked at me with a quizzical look. "Why is he limping?"

"Dunno," I said. "Didn't tell."

* * *

I was up and about in a couple of days. I could move about with a limp but the pain in the ankle was still there. It would be about a week before I could be back at school, the doctor had said.

That, I thought was a small price to pay to be alive.

But Dad now wanted to know exactly what happened. He had given me time to rest and recover. Now he wanted to know the truth.

I told him. His firm tone told me that this was not a moment to offer no comment. That, I felt, would have had some consequences I was not keen to find out.

So I told him.

He stared at me for a few moments and then looked away. I had never seen him that angry – and worried.

"You know you just escaped from a horrible death, don't you?"

I nodded, gulping.

"And we had warned you about exactly this sort of thing happening?"

Again, a nod.

"You think next time you are going to be this lucky?"

I didn't know what to say. I wanted to say that I wouldn't be alive if not for Robbie but somehow I felt that would not be the right thing to say. But Dad seemed to have guessed my thoughts.

"Robbie saved you, yes, we know and we are very grateful for that." He was looking straight at me now. "He is a brave boy, braver than most adults. But if not for him you wouldn't have been in this trouble in the first place."

He got up, the stern expression still darkening his face.

"You are not a little kid anymore. You need to be more careful, especially about your own life. Forget Uni or TAFE or whatever you want to do in the future. You got to be alive to do anything." He paused, as if tired by his own words, or simply by having to say them.

"As we always say, it is your life. You are free to decide whether you want to risk your life again or not."

Then he walked away, leaving me to ponder my future.

I pondered.

Dad I realized, had spoilt the joy I was feeling at having been saved by Robbie, being carried by him, the warmth I felt for his courage, his sacrifice and his concern for me. Since learning that Robbie had saved my life I had been basking in the glow of that knowledge, thrilled to bits to know that Robbie cared for me that much. It had made me forget that I had in fact escaped death by a whisker. Now Dad was reminding me of that, taking the shine off Robbie's bravery and care. But I got to say he had a point. Robbie's courage and sacrifice did not change the fact I had cheated death. A few more seconds and I would have been mincemeat. Or kebab, depending on whether it was the train or the Afghans that got me first. We were lucky the train had come. I was lucky that Robbie was there.

But will we be so lucky the next time?

I knew there would be a next time. Because the Afghans will return and when they do we were gonna to get hurt.

Have things gone too far?

When Robbie bashed people it did not appear that way. We always got away with it. And somehow I did not feel involved. It was always Robbie bashing somebody. Robbie got bashed by Gary but that didn't count. It had become almost normal. This time somebody had come looking for Robbie to take revenge for what he did. And I had been at the receiving end, escaping a horrible death only by whiskers.

And my parents' voice: Robbie may not get away with things all the time.

It did not matter if Robbie saved me. I had still been close to death because of Robbie's violence. Has my hopeless infatuation made me vulnerable to terrible possibilities I had never thought of?

It made me feel something strange and ugly inside me. A dark and cold fear for myself. That was the first time I had felt that since getting to know Robbie.

SEVEN

"If ya don't like hanging with me then just fuck off!"

Robbie spat.

We were walking back home from the movies. That was the first time we had been out since my "accident". Sarah had not turned up – family thing again- but Marty and Mark had been. We had a quiet time, Marty not farting for once. There was little talk about the incident with the Afghans as I guess everybody felt there was nothing to talk about. We just felt scared shitless. At least everybody except Robbie did.

After the movie Robbie suggested that we go to the station and chill for a while. It was still only six o'clock even though it was now pretty dark, it being June. Marty and Mark excused themselves, Marty saying he had footy training and Mark because he had to take his mum to the doctor. But that didn't worry Robbie. He was not happy but he was also determined to go to the station. And as usual, he took it for granted that I, his loyal disciple, would follow him without a question.

But I was not completely thrilled with the idea. After my little chat with Mum and Dad, I had been thinking of how best to avoid another disaster like the one I had escaped. Dad had been his usual Buddhist self, suggesting what I should do without telling me what to do and he seemed to be suggesting that I reconsider my friendship with Robbie. Mum on the other hand was getting increasingly anxious and I could see that she was very unhappy with the way Dad was handling things. "I think he needs to be told things in plain language," she told Dad in my presence after she heard the train story. Then she told me things in plain language. "Very soon", she said, her face like a pappadam, "You will have to find a different group of friends or not have friends at all." She did not say what would happen if I didn't follow her instructions but I was left in no doubt that the pappadam would burst with disastrous consequences for all.

But following her instructions, I thought, was simply impossible. I didn't mind not seeing Marty, Mark and Sarah. But life without Robbie would be no life at all. What do I have to look forward to each day if I am not meeting him?

But, I had also realized by now that life with Robbie could also mean the end of my life. It had almost come to that. Almost. Seeing my parents getting so worried and cranky wasn't good either. I had never seen them so worried and to think that I was the cause of it was not a good feeling.

But the trick I thought was not to ditch Robbie - which I couldn't - but to balance Robbie and safety, which I thought I could.

And that evening came the first chance to do so, after the movie as we were walking back. I had been hoping that Robbie would go somewhere else, anywhere, other than the station but my heart took a dive when Robbie mentioned the station. Heart going steadily weak, I suggested in my meek, feeble way that maybe it was not a good idea, not yet at least. And Robbie took it personally.

"That is where we usually hang out." He affirmed. "No fucken Afghan is gonna change that!"

His face glowed when he spoke. Now I could see the scar on his cheek clearly. It was not one given by Gary, I was sure of that. It was the result of that tortuous trek he had made through the scrub. It wasn't too bad but it scarred his handsome face, and was likely to be there for a few days at least. And it must have stung. Throughout the movie, I had seen him touch it and wince slightly.

He seemed determined to return to the station. We couldn't let the Afghans decide where we met, he insisted. Besides, he argued, it had been a week since we had been there. The Afghans were not likely to be prowling around that long. But I guess the truth was that he was so used to being there, like a second home.

But you can't take a chance, can you? I tried to reason again.

That's when he got angry. If ya don't like hanging out with me then fuck off! As simple as that.

But I knew he really didn't mean it. He was just annoyed, with me, with the Afghans, perhaps with himself as well.

"You know that is not true."

"Yeah?" He sneered. "Don't tell me you are concerned for my safety!"

I said nothing. It was a hard question. I knew I was worried about Robbie's safety but I was also fearful of my own safety now. More than ever. I wasn't sure which fear was greater. I didn't want to find out either.

"We need to be more careful" I said, trying hard to emphasize the we. 'All these fights are only going to backfire on us."

"Don't say we!" Robbie sensed my strategy. He was not just a pretty face. "I am the one who is having fights. You can piss off anytime."

He took a cigarette from his pocket and lit it. I could see his hand shaking slightly.

"Everybody seems to be backing out. You don't need to tag along"

That was a reference to Sarah and the other two. Sarah has not been a regular on the platform lately and tonight Marty and Mark had been less than convincing in their explanations for not coming with us. Perhaps, they too were beginning to see where all this could be leading.

We continued to walk in silence. Robbie smoking, I thinking.

How was I going to get this into Robbie's head? That this is now not a joke anymore?

We were approaching the place where the road split into two, one taking us past the station and the other past the park. My heart was now beginning to pick up its beat. What if we see the Afghans again? What if they see us? What if they are already there, waiting for us? Please Robbie, not the station.

But I was too scared now to tell him again.

We were at the junction now and the light at the station was visible through the trees. My heart was beginning to race.

Then, a surprise. Robbie suddenly turned away from the road that lead to the station and crossed the road. Without waiting to see if I was following, he began walking. He was going towards the park!

My Robbie! The boy with the golden hair and the golden heart!

I followed him, the heart steadily gaining its normal rate and filling with warmth for Robbie. I caught up with him and looked up. Robbie looked straight ahead. Only the red scar, dark and harsh, stared at me in the light of the street lamp.

"Thanks Robbie."

He looked down at me, blowing smoke. The anger was gone now. In its place, pain.

"One day," he said softly, almost to himself. "One day you should change places with me. Just one day! Then you will fucking see!"

* * *

For the next few days, we met at the park. We sat around, Robbie and Marty smoked, we all talked crap. But the crap now was pretty subdued. After the Afghan attack, nobody seemed to have any appetite for talking. We all sat there in the park like shadows in the darkness of the winter evenings, listening to the wind in the trees. Each time a train came in and took off in the distance my heart jumped and every time something moved in the park, a man walking a dog, a solitary jogger, I started.

It was mostly us four boys now. Sarah joined us too but her visits were becoming less regular. And she was getting into arguments with Robbie most of the time. Robbie was convinced she was seeing someone each time she stayed away for a 'family thing', which was now becoming quite frequent. It was as if she had suddenly discovered her family, Robbie once said sarcastically. But Sarah simply did what she wanted.

I guess she was also worried, after the train incident. Robbie, she would have finally realized, was going to make a very dangerous lover, possibly a fatal one. It was best to keep away as much as possible. I am sure Marty and Mark felt the same. They were also offering excuses; footy practice, doctor's appointment, etc. etc..

Even homework! Apart from being fuckwits they were also selfish pricks. They would suck up to Robbie only as long as it didn't put them in danger. I guess I was the only one who still wanted to be with Robbie even though with some safety precautions.

Yes, things may not have been as good as they had been but I was at least relieved that we were not at the station. It did not feel completely safe in the park but at least safer than the platform. I wouldn't have been too worried about Mark and Marty or even Sarah not being there too often for that matter but not Robbie. He was not happy with the way things were turning out. If anything he was getting more restless. He was getting pissed off at Sarah too often and yelling at Marty and Mark for not spending more time at the park. He did not yell at me but he was often sharp and abrupt with me. I guess he was not feeling comfortable at the park, kinda out of place. Maybe he was also realizing that things were not the same anymore, that something, somewhere was changing, without him not knowing what to do about it.

Besides, after a short respite, Gary was becoming violent again.

One evening Robbie came with a big black spot on the right side of his face, eyes red and cheeks flushed. Only I was at the park to see it and I was not going to ask the cause of it. It was not a punch on, I could see that. I had been with Robbie long enough to know the difference between the bruises he got from fights and the damage caused by Gary. That evening nobody else came and I sat with him, in silence for nearly an hour, listening to the crickets in the bushes and Robbie sobbing, longing to hug the heaving shoulders but not having the courage, feeling the hopelessness of having a crush on a straight guy.

And Robbie too was getting more violent.

He had a particularly nasty fight with a big Islander kid one evening at the mall. He beat the Islander pretty badly but also received a swollen lip and a bloody nose, one of the very few times Robbie had got bruised by someone other than Gary. The old scar which was healing well got opened and he was in agony. We sat in the park and Sarah tried to wash the bruises with water.

"Shit, you're hurting me!" Robbie groaned. "You don't know how to do it. Give it to Shehan!" He ordered. Sarah swore loudly and handed me the water bottle and the handkerchief. "Don't ask me to wipe your shit again," she fired as she walked away and sat on the grass, grumpy as ever. Robbie winced as I washed the wound but said nothing. I could not see if he was crying because it was too dark.

Certainly things were not improving for Robbie. If anything they were going downhill.

*　*　*

Robbie was not the only one unhappy about the way things were going. My parents were also not impressed. When Dad heard that I was still hanging out with Robbie he didn't say anything but raised his eyebrows and looked at Mum who raised her eyebrows even more. I guess they were disappointed that the philosophical approach had not worked, and Mum in particular seemed to be pretty unhappy about it. They both settled down a bit when I said we were not meeting at the station anymore but I could see that the worry was there. However, they stuck to their old ways. At least Dad did.

"Well," he said. "We have done our bit. The rest is up to you. But don't say we didn't warn you!"

That night, I heard my parents arguing after a long time. I guess this is what happens when the eye communication breaks down. The last time I had seen something even close to this happen was years ago when they could not decide whether they should send some money to Dad's brother in Galle or his sister in Matara. Mum thought the Matara family deserved it more but Dad disagreed. The result was a big argument. I never thought charity could arouse so much passion in my normally calm parents. But that passion was nowhere close to what they were showing now. This time the argument was about me, their only child.

"I really think we have been too lenient with Shehan," I heard Mum say in the kitchen. Her voice sounded annoyed, the kind of annoyance people have when they are finally fed up with something they have put up with for a long time. She was trying to keep her voice down for fear of me overhearing. But she didn't have to. I was already outside my room in the dark listening.

"Your philosophy is not working anymore. He is back to where he was, with Robbie."

"Not really," I heard my smartass Dad say. "He is back with Robbie but now they are in the park."

I am sure Mum would have made a face that would have chased a thousand ships. I only heard her though.

"You are still joking about this. This is our boy we are talking about. He had just escaped death and he is back with the boy who nearly got him killed! And you are joking about it!"

Her voice was angry now, getting louder and shaking.

"He is infatuated with that boy. Following him around wherever he goes. It's going way too far."

"What do you want me to do? Ground him? Lock him in a room?" Now Dad was getting a bit worked up.

"No, you can at least be more firm with him," Mum was carrying on. I heard the plates clattering in the sink and realized she was nervous.

"One of these days he will come home with something much worse than a sprained ankle and then you will see where your philosophy has taken him!"

I guess that was a bit too much for Dad, even with his philosophical mind. I heard him get up with a start.

"Oh, why don't you go give it some rest! I am sick of this whinging!"

I have never heard Dad speaking to Mum like that, in that tone and so loudly. Even when they had that previous argument years ago there was no shouting like this, just loud debate, parliamentary style. This time it was pretty serious, I could tell. And I could also feel that this was not the start of the argument. Obviously they have been discussing this when I wasn't there, and probably Mum had been bugging Dad a lot about his philosophical leniency.

Mum was saying something loudly and I heard Dad coming upstairs, his feet falling heavily on the steps. I quickly made my way to the room. I did not hear the rest of the conversation, or argument. I guess I had heard enough anyway.

That night for the first time in my life I heard Mum cry. Not loudly but she was sobbing, I could say. I heard the loud sniffles from next door and I tell you it was like hearing it inside my own head, tearing and squeezing it.

I spent a long time thinking that night. Things were indeed getting a bit out of hand. The sound of my Mum sobbing was an indication that things were worse than I had ever imagined.

Suddenly it seemed that I had landed in a world of shit and the shit was getting thicker all the time, pulling everybody into it. I felt uneasy like I had never felt in my life. Restless. Troubled. Long after Mum's sobbing had ceased I kept tossing and turning in bed, thinking and wondering.

What had happened to the magical life I had last summer, fawning over Robbie, spending hours at the station watching trains and life pass by without any worry or concern? It was gone, like a train that was there on the platform for just a few seconds and I was left in the darkness with the sound of my parents screaming at each other.

I did not know how I could pull myself out of this shit before I got completely drowned in it. I only knew that I had to.

I knew I could not go back to the life of last summer. It was gone. That much was clear. I had to look forward, a way to move on from here without more trouble. I had already created enough trouble for myself and my parents. I didn't want to add to that.

I continued to think. One of the ways I could get out of this, I figured, would be to start focusing on my studies. It was still not too late to get a respectable ATAR and set myself up for a decent Uni course, whatever that may be. That would give me the chance at a secure, safe future. That would also make my parents happier.

But what about Robbie?

I did not know what I should do about him. I did not want to lose him. A life without Robbie seemed pretty boring and empty, no matter what my parents thought about him.

But I didn't want to be like him either. I got to admit I was getting worried about him. Seriously. It was not just the near-death experience. Watching him sit there in the park, cranky and argumentative, sometimes crying, sometimes bleeding, made me realise, I guess perhaps for the first time since meeting him, what a bad shape he was really in. He was lost. Truly. Running away from Gary, running away from the Afghans, and nothing really to run away to except that dark park where he yelled at his girlfriend and cursed his friends. It was not something I wanted for myself.

Funny isn't it? Robbie was my hero but I didn't want to be like him.

But then, I didn't want Robbie to be like that either. I wanted my hero to rule the world but he was constantly being beaten by that world. I did not want that for him. But I could not do anything to change it. I was used to just being there for him, following him, not telling him what to do. Not that he would listen to anyone telling him how to live his life. The only time he had changed something was when he decided to go to the park instead of the station that evening. And I know he did that for me, not for himself.

So I guess I was thinking, that if I could not change him, I would not be like him.

I felt I was being forced to make a difficult decision. Robbie or my future. If I hung out with Robbie I may end up like him. If I didn't hang out with Robbie I may lose him. But I did not want to lose him. He was still my hero, my Robbie, even if it meant that by clinging to him I too could get drowned by life. I could not imagine a life without him. But I did not want to lose my life with him either.

So I made a decision.

If Robbie did not change, I will. But I will also keep Robbie.

Easier said than done? My dad always says everything is impossible in this world until you try.

I will try. My best.

EIGHT

The change came sooner than I expected. And in a way I could have never predicted.

For a few days after that argument, my parents left me alone. There were no further inquiries about me hanging out with Robbie. But their conversation with me was minimal and usually in that monotone that I hate. Just the monotone, not even gentle sarcasm. It was as if they were trying to give me the impression that as far as they were concerned I could still do whatever I liked but unlike those days now they didn't give a shit. I knew they did but it hurt when they pretended they didn't, which I guess was what they wanted me to feel in the first place. The fact that I was now spending more time doing homework did not seem to matter to them. I was still spending time with Robbie and the gang but I was also staying up till late, catching up on my work, waking up to a perpetual yawn the following morning. But that did not seem to register with them, perhaps because as far as they were concerned, it did not matter how much time I spent with my books if I was also spending time with Robbie.

Mum and Dad were speaking to each other but I realized there was still a lot of tension between them. Now they were using that monotone with each other as well.

At school, exams were getting closer and SACs were piling up. English, Math, Physics, Chem. When I ended up with 47% for a Methods SAC, the lowest I had ever received, I realized that things were indeed more serious than I thought.

My parents who had been trying to show that they had given up on me now suddenly dropped all pretensions. We had another one of those family meetings in the lounge after dinner.

Mum and Dad sat with tight faces that seemed as if they had forgotten how to smile and were waiting for somebody to remind them. For a moment I toyed with the idea of obliging them but lacked the main ingredient for the job: courage.

"Well," started Dad. "What do you have to say about this?" He was waving the SAC in the air in front of my face. Boy, he was getting really serious now. From the corner of my eye, I saw Mum looking at me as if daring me to make a smart-ass remark.

"I guess I will have to work harder," was all I could say.

Dad was not impressed. "Of course, you will work harder," he said as if not working harder was not an option. The philosophy seems to have gone out of the window.

"You will work harder and we will help you," Mum said. "Dad knows a good tutor who is supposed to be one of the best in the subject. He can arrange for you to attend his classes"

He conducted group classes, once a week on a Thursday evening, Mum said. No more than four people to a class and he had a reputation for being a man who got everybody study scores higher than 45. People reserved him at least a year in advance, but Dad got special consideration because he works on the guy's car.

"Would you like to go to him and improve your math?" Dad

asked. Now he seemed to be going back to his philosophical ways, giving me a choice. "Of course, you don't have to if you don't want to. It's your life and your responsibility."

I looked at him to see if his philosophy matched his mood and found a stern pair of eyes looking at me.

"However, I must suggest in the strongest possible terms that you take this class and see how you go."

Yes, I realized. I was right the first time. Philosophy had given way to reality.

I agreed. I had to. That 47% was hard to erase from my mind. Plus, I didn't want to find out how Dad would react if I didn't.

That Wednesday I told the gang that I had a tuition class the following evening from 6.30 till 8.30. "I may not be able to make it tomorrow night," I said weakly, glancing at Robbie.

We were sitting in the park as usual. It was one of those days when everybody was there, now gradually becoming less and less frequent. Robbie was leaning against the pillar, one dirty-sneak-ered foot on the bench, the other on the ground, a fag in his mouth. Sarah sat with her back to him, leaning against his leg and we, the disciples of the great Robbie sat on the ground. Marty was sipping a coke.

"Why the fuck does the class go for that long?" Mark asked, looking at me sideways.

I shrugged my shoulders. "That's the normal session."

Robbie glanced down at me, blowing a puff of smoke.

"Cantcha get here after the class?"

I pursed my lips. "Yeah, I guess so." But I knew that would be pushing it.

"Then get your ass down here after the class. We'll still be here." He glanced at Marty as if daring him to contradict him. Marty just looked away at the darkness.

I nodded. It would be at least nine by the time I got here and I would be pretty tired I was sure. Not to mention hungry. And what if there was homework? How will Mum and Dad, in their new stern mood, feel about me going straight to Robbie from the class? But I nodded, not game enough to contradict Robbie.

"So you're really gunning for a high ATAR huh?" Marty again.

"Yeah, I guess."

"You wanna go to Uni and shit?"

"I guess."

I saw Robbie look away.

"Oh, ok," Marty said, not very concerned.

"Then you will not be hanging out with us anymore I guess," Sarah said, casually. Robbie had pulled her to him now, his arms around her and Sarah was playing with the bracelet in his arm. It was nice to see her in this mood after a long time. Seemed like old times.

"Don't talk rubbish," I said, annoyed. It seemed silly to think that I would want to stay away from Robbie. But there was something else silly about it. I suddenly realized that she was talking about this lifestyle continuing for a long time into the future. This lifestyle of sitting around and talking crap. Six months ago that would not have moved me. But now the realization made me shudder.

Robbie wasn't impressed with my response "Bullshit!" He spat. "Bullshit! You will come here a day, maybe two and then it will be once a week, once a month and then never again."

"Come on Robbie, you know I will never do that!"

I wanted to sound convincing but I felt something beginning to pull me back.

Robbie said nothing. He threw the fag end on the grass.

"Which Uni you wanna go to?" Sarah asked.

"Dunno," I said, looking at Robbie who was staring at the tracks. His mood was getting spoilt rapidly, I could see.

"Monash, maybe Melbourne."

"Which one's better?"

"Dunno. Dad says Melbourne is more prestigious and shit. But I really dunno."

"My dad says I should go to Uni too but I don't think I got the brains for it," Sarah said and laughed. Marty looked at her as if the mere thought was a joke.

Robbie pushed Sarah away and sat up. "I am sick of this crap," he said without looking at anybody. "Let's go!"

Sarah, now increasingly the reluctant consort, got up after him. Robbie grabbed her hand and they walked towards the gate.

"Make sure you get here tomorrow!" He instructed as he walked away, without looking back.

I went home somewhat deflated. The whole episode bothered me; Sarah expecting life to continue as it did, Robbie's forceful tone, almost ordering me to be there despite my class. It had never quite bothered me in the past. In fact ,I kind of liked it, Robbie demonstrating his authority. But that evening something made me feel less than satisfied, almost irritated. Was it because I was now beginning to get interested in my own future? Was I even finally getting tired of Robbie?

No! I cried inwardly. It cannot happen. It will not happen.

* * *

The class was at the tutor's house, about 15 minutes from where we lived. When I got there the others were already there. A girl, a brown-haired little thing called Katherine and two boys, an

Aussie boy called James and Harsha, a thin twiggy Indian whose nickname I later learned to my pleasant surprise was also Twiggy.

The tutor, Mr. Ganesh, was a little grey-haired Indian man with a perpetually troubled look on his face. Perhaps he had spent too long solving math problems, I thought as I sat down next to Twiggy. We all shared little nods and smiles before Ganesh got down to business.

The lesson itself was useful but boring. I could not suppress my yawns and once or twice I saw Katherine glancing at me and smiling mischievously. James too was stifling a yawn. Twiggy alone stared at the mouth of Ganesh as if his life depended on it.

At the end of the class we got out of the house. We were all catching trains although in different directions. I was going south to Robbie and the rest going home to parents.

We walked to the station, chatting, getting to know each other. James I found was pretty intelligent and very talkative. Good-looking in a nerdish sort of way, he was also a bit of a brag-gart. He boasted about his new phone as if he was the only one who had one. Twiggy on the other hand was not the nerd he ap-peared to be. He played basketball for his school and had a black belt in Judo. I asked him whether the belt was to hold the judo costume together. A lame and cruel joke but they all laughed, in-cluding Twiggy who it appeared also had a good sense of humor.

Katherine was a quiet little thing. She laughed at my belt joke – and a few others – but said little else. Her parents were quite religious, the kind that spent a lot of time at the church and with the church. She too went to church every Sunday. But that was mainly because she liked to sing the hymns, she said cheekily.

It was the first time I had been with another group of people my age for a long time. They were an interesting bunch of peo-ple. Very different to my gang.

It was nearly 9.15 by the time I got to the park. I had not noticed but we had taken our time taking a leisurely walk up to the station. There was nobody at the park near the bench, only shadows hovering in the dark.

"Where the fuck have you been?" one of the shadows barked. It was Marty. He came out of the shadows where he had been sitting. He was alone too.

"Where are the others?" I asked.

"Gone," he said, simply. 'They waited for you till nine and guessed you were not coming. Robbie was really pissed off."

I said nothing. I didn't feel good. That was for sure.

Marty yawned. "I don't know what's wrong with him now," he said, obviously referring to Robbie. "Way too cranky now. Not like those days." He yawned again. "I am heading home." He said, already on his way out. "Catch ya."

* * *

"How was the class?" Dad asked when I got home.

"Oh pretty cool," I said. "He is very good."

"I told you!"

There was a pause as I opened the fridge looking for something to drink.

"Did you come straight home?"

"Yeah," I said. "Tired."

I did feel truly tired that night. In body and mind. I was tired of having sat there in the class for two hours. And I was worried about missing Robbie. I had texted him apologizing for the delay but had received no reply.

It was the first time I had missed Robbie. Whenever we were to meet I had always made it, shower or shine, whether the others were there or not. It annoyed me that I missed him this time. But strangely, it also annoyed me that he was so pissed off with me for that. After all, this was the first time and I had a good reason for it. What did he expect me to do? Give up my studies?

I guess I didn't realise it then but I was changing. Slowly but surely. Becoming more and more concerned about my own future. My irritation with Robbie was only the first sign. More was to come pretty soon.

NINE

That spring what would have seemed like the impossible happened.

I fell in love. With a girl!

The girl was Katherine. Well, maybe it was not exactly love. Maybe it was lust, at least at the start. It's hard to tell at the start of a crush.

I was getting along well with her, getting to know her and becoming comfortable with her, my first real female acquaintance. Of course, there was Sarah but she was like Robbie's girl and nothing else to anybody. She treated us as Robbie's friends and without Robbie we were nothing to her, I am sure. Katherine was different. She was a girl who was a separate individual, not attached to anybody and a girl with a warm personality I could really connect with. She was quiet and intelligent and she liked my jokes. Besides, a couple of weeks into the math classes I had also noticed that Katherine had one of the most rounded asses I had ever seen on anybody. I swear they were round. Perfectly round especially when she wore jeans. I had noticed them the very first evening but they became more and more obvious, as if they were getting rounder and fuller each time I saw her. And each time I sat next to her, which was becoming a habit now, I felt this strange stirring all over me, like a current, something I had only felt before on that very first day when Robbie sat next to me in class and after that frequently when I was with Robbie. Now it was happening with Katherine. And the groin wasn't perfectly still either. Before I knew what was happening I was having awkward moments in my seat.

"Shehan, stop squirming and finish your work."

Ganesh would command looking more worried than usual. Katherine would glance at me and smile cheekily. Did she know? Those big brown eyes said yes.

But I wanted to make sure and one day, deciding to be bolder than I had ever been in my life I reached under the table and squeezed her thigh. There was no response. The little thing didn't even look at me. I was sitting there thinking shit I have made an ass of myself when, just a few moments later, a little hand slipped under the table and prodded my crotch. I glanced up long enough to catch a glimpse of a wink.

That girl had more cheek than I imagined.

That was the beginning. That evening after class I let Twiggy and James walk to the station saying Dad was picking me up and Katherine, the intelligent being, realized I wanted to talk and made a similar excuse. Then we talked, standing outside Ganesh's house ignoring Ganesh and his little wife who were throwing suspicious looks at us from the verandah. I told her that I was shocked by her groping and she said that she was shocked by what she had groped. It was all tongue in cheek, good healthy flirting, something I had never done in my life and I was liking it. Robbie had never flirted with me. I had simply fawned on him.

And that night I found my hands straying down to the hardness between my legs, trying to recapture the magic I had felt when that little hand prodded it in the evening. But somewhere within a little voice was trying to scream: This is not right! You have Robbie! But the voice was too faint. The hand did not hear it.

Afterwards, I lay there feeling all shitty about what I had done. I felt like I had betrayed Robbie and committed adultery. I tried to sleep it off but I couldn't. Around midnight the hardness was back and this time I did not hear the little voice.

Very soon we were meeting on days when we had no class. A couple of times for a pizza, once or twice to the movies where there was a lot of groping. I also had my first kiss, a long tongue twister that smelt of mustard from the hotdogs we had just had but felt like a firebomb had gone off in my belly. By now it was turning into something more than pure lust. I knew it because when I came after meeting her, my heart felt like my groin. On fire.

* * *

My parents noticed the difference very soon. They are parents, for god's sake.

"Everything alright?" Dad asked noticing how moody I was getting now. "Nah," I said. "Just tired." As if I could hoodwink the old smartass.

And Robbie noticed too.

Since I was experiencing the stirrings in my groin at the sight and thought of Kathryn I had missed a few meetings with Robbie and the gang. They were back at the station now. Robbie had decreed that as it was now weeks since the Afghan attack they were not likely to be prowling around the station anymore. Naturally, we all followed but I was now not the diehard regular anymore. At first, Robbie was really pissed off. He yelled at me, asking if I was a part of the group anymore. "If you aren't then fuck off!" He would hiss. I would cringe but say nothing. I knew he would cool down soon and didn't really mean for me to fuck off. And I was right. As he realized that I was still going to turn up but not every evening we met, he soon settled down as if resigned to the fact.

I didn't realise it then but the group was slowly breaking up. Marty and Mark were not coming as frequently as they used to and Sarah was becoming rarer and rarer. I later realized that sometimes it must have been just Robbie, sitting there in the dark, waiting for friends. But at the time it did not cross my mind. I had other things to occupy it. Hell, I was not even all that worried about Robbie getting pissed off at me anymore. Suddenly he was not the centre of my world. Now there was Kathy.

But I still felt a part of the group. I did not want to leave it. I did not want to leave Robbie. At least that's what I told myself. But I guess now with my newfound love and confidence I also wanted to show that I was my own man. So I went to my classes, went to the movies with Kathy and went to the station when I got the time.

* * *

And when I realized that my fancy for Kathy was not something passing and that it had a lot more to it than a rampant groin, I told my parents. They had a right to know, I thought. And they would be pleased to know that their son was capable of thinking lustfully about someone other than Robbie. And I knew they would be thrilled to know that it was a girl.

"You are in what? Dad asked, looking up from his plate of rice.

"In love, I think. With a girl."

My Dad raised his eyebrows and looked at Mum who was showing that she could do it even better. The eye communication was now back to normal.

"Well," Dad said, lowering the eyebrows. "It had to happen I guess. Who is the girl?"

"She is in my tuition class."

"Oh, that one!" He smiled knowingly. He had seen Kathy a few times when he came to pick me up.

"I am sure it's for the best," Mum said. "But make sure you do your tuition well"

Then I got bolder. I told Robbie.

His reaction was totally different.

"Girl friend?" He asked. Well, almost growled, his thick, full lips churning out the word like something toxic. He looked half amused and half annoyed, as if not sure which emotion to choose.

"Yes," I said. "A girlfriend."

Now the amusement in the eyes disappeared as he realized that it was for real. Then annoyance took over.

"You got a girlfriend?"

He laughed. Usually, it so fucking hot when he laughs but now I found it annoying. The mockery sounded like mockery.

"Yes," I said, trying to assert myself. "I got a girlfriend and a hot one."

Robbie wanted to laugh more but the anger welling in him prevented it.

"You can't even get a guy, how can you get a girl?"

"I can get girls and I have got one!"

Boy, this was a bit too much I thought. All this time I had a crush on him he would show no interest. Now he was pissed off because I had found a girl of my own. I guess I was too blinded at the time with my lust for Kathy to see what it really meant.

"You fucking fag! Girls don't fall for little fags like you."

I got up. I had had enough.

"Where the fuck are you going?"

"Home! I have a home!"

Shit. That was the wrong thing to say. To Robbie, especially when he was in this state. But as I said, I was blind.

Before I knew it Robbie was up and his hand was grabbing me by the front of my t-shirt.

"Say it again Fag! Say it again!"

I was terrified. I tell you I had seen Robbie in a rage many times but had never thought I'd see the day he flew into a rage against me. I was too terrified to speak.

"Say it!"

I didn't.

Then he hit me. Not a straight-out punch but a thundering smack on the side of my face. I guess he reserved his punches for real men. Fags like me he just smacked.

But it was enough. I reeled and fell. The side of my face stung. I could feel tears bursting inside my eyes. I looked up and saw Robbie looking down at me. There was anger and hurt in those eyes. And something else. It took me a long time to figure out what it was. But at the time I saw nothing but his rage. Felt nothing but my own fear and outrage.

I got up and without looking back, walked away.

"Fuck off!" I heard him yell. "Fuck off to your bitch girlfriend you fucking faggot!"

He was screaming. Strangely the voice was not angry anymore. Well, it was, but it was breaking at the edge.

When I came home with a blood smeared face and broken lip my parents were worried.

"What happened?"

"Nothing," I said. "I slipped and fell."

"You must find something more original," Dad said, grinning. "What happened?"

I told them. I told them that I had an argument with Robbie and that he smacked me. I am done with him, I said. Forever. No more Robbie.

It was true. When I walked away from the station I had decided never to see him again. I will never have anything to do with someone who wanted to treat me like the people he bashed. I didn't need him anymore. I had Kathy.

If Dad's sigh of relief was audible, Mum's was almost deafening.

"Good decision." She said, firmly. "Seems like you learnt your lesson, the hard way."

Yeah, I thought. The hard way. And I was glad that it was just a split lip.

<h1 style="text-align:center">TEN</h1>

I did not see Robbie again for a long time. And when I saw him that was under very different circumstances.

For the next few weeks, I was preoccupied with studies and Kathy. We studied together and during breaks between model English and physics papers, I finally figured out that after all, it was more love than just lust. I brought her home and she took me to meet her parents. They were cool people. Her dad taught Religious Education in the same school Kathy went to and her mum stayed at home. They were very religious but not the kind that pushed their religion down others' throats, least of all their daughter's. Like my parents, they too knew that a healthy relationship was important to a teenager. And to the delight of my mum, they both liked curry.

I now had a new group of friends, James, Twiggy and a whole bunch of others, guys and girls I had got to know through them. They were great people, fun to be with, safe to be with and above all, high achievers. Their enthusiasm for academic excellence was rubbing off on me and I loved the feeling. Life indeed was good.

I heard little from Robbie. That night, after the beating, he had tried to call me on my mobile. I saw his number. But I had turned the phone off. I didn't want to speak to him anymore, I had decided. It was not likely that he would call home but if he did I had told Mum and Dad to tell him I was away.

The following evening he texted me" Where the fck r u?" I didn't answer. Didn't even say FO.

Two more messages and he too fell silent.

I soon lost touch with the rest of the gang. Marty left school to take up an apprenticeship. Mark stayed on, focusing more on footy than his studies. And I went on focusing on studies and Kathy.

I did not hear much about Robbie at all. Once Mark told me that he had met him, that he was still at the station, alone, smoking a fag. Even Sarah wasn't there, he said. He didn't know where she was or what she was doing now. He had heard that they had broken up but he wasn't sure. Robbie looked fine, he said. He had shown little interest in chatting though. Mark had walked away after failing to engage Robbie in a conversation.

There were also rumours that the Afghans were prowling around again. There was another rumour that Silvio was also looking for him, with a new-found gang, to avenge his humiliation more than a year ago.

I felt sorry for Robbie, sitting there all alone. I even thought about contacting him again but didn't. Why go back to the past, I thought. I had made a clean break with the past, with Robbie, with the gang. Everything had worked well for me. I had a great girl, my studies were going well, and I was looking at an ATAR in the high eighties. Why spoil all that? If Robbie had issues he should deal with them, just like I did.

It was only later that I recognised how simple-minded I was, how blind, how selfish. I should have seen it then, that day on the platform by the rail tracks where Robbie smacked me. I could not figure it out then, what I saw in his eyes when he looked down at me. I thought it was rage, pure rage and perhaps jealousy too. Robbie was consumed by anger at what I was having and what he could never have.

Now I see it clearly. It was not just rage, not just jealousy. They were there, yes, in large doses. But there was something else welling in those big blue eyes. It was fear. Pure, undiluted fear. The fear of losing me, his friend, his only friend and the terror of being alone in the world. Forever. He just couldn't say it in words.

And when I finally saw it, it was too late.

It was the day the results were released. As expected I had a high ATAR of 89.9. Kathy did way better. 98.9

Our parents were thrilled. My dad was organising the biggest curry bash in that side of town that night and Kathy's parents too were invited. As for Kathy and me, we had a lot more on our minds than munching curry. But we attended the dinner and soon excused ourselves. We wanted to party with our friends, my new friends, the high achievers, and we were gonna party well into the night.

It must have been past midnight when I received the call. It was Dad and he sounded worried. He had called me several times but I had not picked up. I probably did not hear the phone ringing because of the noise in the bar. But now that I had finally picked it up he had some bad news for me.

"It's Robbie." He said. His voice was shaking. "He's in hospital"

Robbie! In hospital? Why?

There was a pause at the other end. Then my father's voice, small and weak.

"Apparently he has been bashed."

I felt my legs go weak and my head swimming. Robbie bashed! Gary must have finally stepped over the line.

I rushed to the hospital with Kathy. My parents were already there.

"They found him at the station. Beside the tracks." Dad said. "Doctors say it's touch and go."

I walked into the ward as if in a dream, floating up to the bed in the corner.

Robbie lay in the bed wrapped in bandages. Both arms were in casts, one leg suspended, metal pins holding something to his head. His face was the only part of him that was visible. That angelic face that had driven me crazy smeared with blood, the eyes closed.

A nurse whispered that we were not to speak to him. I wasn't going to do it anyway. I couldn't. There was something big and heavy stuck in my throat.

Then Robbie opened his eyes. Those big blue eyes opened one more time and looked at me. I could feel Kathy's hand clutching mine and I squeezed it, the lump in my throat growing.

His eyes remained open for a few seconds, looking at me. They looked tired and filled with emotions. Raw and pure. Sadness, fear, pain and perhaps a hint of resignation. Unlike on that last day at the station, I recognized them all. Clearly.

"Robbie," I whispered. But only the lips moved. The words died before they were out.

His lips tried to move. Then gave up. The eyes closed.

That was the last time I saw him, alive.

* * *

It was later that morning that we pieced the story together, much of it anyway. I was right. Gary had finally crossed the line. But it had also tipped Robbie over the edge, finally. They found Gary's body in the flat, bashed beyond recognition. His mother too was in bad shape but that was Gary's handiwork. Little Megan was found hiding under the bed, so petrified she could not speak for days.

Robbie was found at the station, beside the railway tracks. Apparently he had been bashed there. But who did it? Gary was already dead by then and other than Gary there were only two other parties who could have bashed Robbie like that. The Afghans and Silvio's gang. Did they finally get him?

I checked my phone and among the many missed calls from Dad that night there were two calls from another number. I had erased Robbie's name from the phonebook weeks ago, but I still remembered it. He had called me twice, within a few seconds, close to midnight. Was it when he was about to get bashed? Or was it when he had got out of the flat after bashing Gary? I could not say and I will never know.

But I know the hospital got in touch with Dad because he had my number in his phone. There had been only two numbers. One was my mobile. The other was my home number.

The funeral was a modest affair. My parents took charge of it. There was nobody else to do it. Robbie's mum was still in bad shape. He had no one else. No family. No friends.

He looked so handsome, as always. Dressed in a suit for the first time, face scrubbed and that blond hair brushed. He looked like any teenager would look in his Formal. Studly. Except this was his funeral.

And when they took the body away they played the song Turn! Turn!! Turn!!!

For everything, there is a season under the heavens.....

That was my dad's idea. The smartass always wanting to make a philosophical statement.

* * *

Now a year later sitting here on the lawn at Uni with Kathy sitting next to me in the sun I wonder what it was all about. Why did it happen? Did it have to happen?

People walk past us, sit around and chat, study, laugh. Young people, bright people with a lot to look forward to, careers, families, happiness.

Robbie could have been anyone of them. I could imagine him with a satchel over his shoulder, dressed in tight jeans, blond as ever, chatting up girls. I could picture him of an evening running past us in his jogging shorts, panting, sweat pouring from his handsome brow. I could see him dancing the night away at the bar down the street girls and guys ogling his blond magnificence.

But it was not to be. It all ended by the railway tracks where he lived most of his life. No Uni, no family, no happiness for him. Killed like a dog.

Why did it happen? Did it have to happen?

I cannot stop blaming myself for what happened to him. I couldn't help him yes, but would things have been that bad if I had not cut him off? I was too blinded by selfishness, I kept telling myself.

My dad thinks it was a tragedy we could not have avoided. Nobody could help him, he said. There are people like that, trapped into lives they cannot escape from. Lives which are vicious holes of filth and violence. The only way you can escape them is through death.

Is he right? Was it why in those last moments Robbie's eyes had a glint of resignation? Maybe it was not resignation. Maybe it was relief. Relief that the torture was finally over.

True, Robbie was a violent boy. He bashed people. He killed his own father for fuck's sake! But his father was already dead a long time ago from something only he knew. And he killed Robbie long before the Afghans got him, by infecting the boy with a vicious, violent monster.

But that is not how I like to remember him. I like to remember him as a good boy, a sweet boy. I like to remember the playful Robbie, the teasing Robbie, the gentle Robbie. The Robbie that made me laugh and the Robbie that made me quiver. The Robbie that carried me all the way from the tracks, wincing from his lacerated arms and face, and his own sprained leg.

I have no pictures of him. Not even a picture on my phone. I erased them all in that fit of rage. But I don't need pictures to remember him. I have many images of him in my head. The best is him in our garden the day I turned the hose on him. I can still picture him standing on the lawn, face between a scowl and a smile, the moment before anger gives way to joy, the body wet and the singlet clinging to his torso. Erotic. Beautiful. Fucking priceless.

That is how I like to remember him.

We are all reborn, my father says. And according to Kathy's dad, there is somebody up there who weighs our good against the bad. I only hope that when Robbie is reborn he will be born close to where I am. And I know that when they weigh his good and bad his good is gonna be so fucking heavy that it will break the fucking scales. If not, God can go to hell.